Glam Squad
&GROOMSMEN

The Enchanted Bridal Series Book Four

D1518391

SAMANTHA CHASE

Copyright © 2018 Samantha Chase

All rights reserved.

ISBN: 978-1985766020

Copyright 2018 Samantha Chase

All Rights Reserved.

No part of this book, with the exception of brief quotations for book reviews or critical articles, may be reproduced or transmitted in any form or by an means, electronic or mechanical, including photocopying, recording, or by any information storage and retrieval system without express written permission from the author.

This is a work of fiction. Names, characters, places, and incidents are the product of the author's imagination or are used fictitiously, and any resemblance to actual persons, living or dead, business establishments, events, or locales is entirely coincidental.

ISBN: 978-1985766020

Editor: Jillian Rivera
Cover artist: Dana Lamothe/Designs by Dana
Print formatting: Kim Brooks

Glam Squad

& GROOMSMEN

ONE

Friday nights at Enchanted Bridal were always crazy, but this was the first time that Penny Blake found herself literally running from the room.

"*Oof!*"

"You okay?"

Looking up, she saw one of her bosses – Angie – standing in front of her.

"Oh, God…sorry," she murmured. When Angie didn't say anything and just continued to study her, Penny knew she needed to explain herself. "I…I um…I just needed to…"

"Pee? Do you need to get to the bathroom?"

"What?" Penny croaked slightly and then immediately cleared her throat. "Um…I mean, no. No, I don't need to use the restroom."

One perfectly-shaped brow arched at her. "What's going on? Is something wrong? Did someone say something to upset you?"

Knowing there was no way to avoid this

conversation, she let out a weary sigh. "You see that woman over there?" She motioned over her shoulder. "Long black hair, black skinny jeans, ivory sweater?"

Angie nodded.

"See the guy with her?"

Angie's eyes widened for a moment before she gave a knowing smile. "The sexy, nerdy guy? Sure. What's up? Is he an ex?"

Penny nodded.

"Damn. Now that is a shame because he's really…"

"Yeah, I know. Trust me."

"So he's here with his fiancée and you'd rather not see him. Got it," Angie said with a quick nod.

"Actually, that's his sister. We used to be friends," Penny said quietly even as she was eyeing the door to the dressing room. Tonight was one of Enchanted Bridal's weekly fashion shows and she was wearing a wedding gown – so even if it wasn't horrifying enough running into your ex-boyfriend, the whole looking-like-a-bride thing just made it even more awkward.

"Used to be? What happened?" Then Angie gasped. "Did she stop being your friend because you broke up with her brother? Was she pissed? Did she hate the two of you dating? Oh my gosh, I know what that's like. I dated a friend's brother and she did not like it one bit. We stopped talking. I wonder whatever happened to her…"

Clearly she wasn't going to make the quick getaway she'd been hoping for.

"Eva never had a problem with Spencer and I

dating. But over the years we just…I don't know…drifted apart. I think things were a little awkward for a while, but we got over it."

"And the whole drifting apart thing…?" Angie prompted.

Penny stared longingly at the exit and wished she had simply kept walking and let her boss follow her. Now she was stuck in a conversation she'd rather not have, all the while hoping Eva and Spencer didn't see her.

Angie glanced over Penny's shoulder. "So you really need to just go and hide out for a few, right?"

Penny nodded. "If that's all right. I hate being a coward or shirking my responsibilities, but if I could just have a few minutes to…"

"Penny? Is that you?"

Angie's face mirrored her own. A little shock, a little *uh-oh*.

But then she grinned. And if Penny didn't like her so much she'd smack her because she had a feeling her boss knew exactly what was going to happen and purposely kept her from hiding.

Dammit.

Turning, Penny forced a smile on her face even as her heart kicked hard in her chest.

"I'm going to want details," Angie whispered so only Penny could hear right before she walked away.

"Oh, my God! It is you! Hi!" Eva cried as she grabbed Penny in a fierce hug. "We saw you up on the stage and I couldn't believe it was you!" Another tight squeeze. "It's been years! Way too long!"

"Uh-huh," Penny murmured, on the verge of gasping for air.

"What are the odds of running into you here? Oh my gosh!" And yet another tight squeeze.

Luckily, she wasn't facing Spencer so she had a minute to collect herself and prepare for all the crazy feelings she got whenever he was near.

"Hey, Eva," Penny said as they finally pulled apart. "It's good to see you. How are you?"

"I'm good, I'm good! And I'm engaged!" she cried as she held up her left hand.

"Congratulations! When's the big day?"

"Sooner than I planned," Eva admitted. "Brett's a Marine and he's shipping out in three months so we moved up our wedding date. I'm hoping to find something off-the-rack that I love and be able to have a somewhat normal wedding."

"I'm sure you'll find something here," Penny said pleasantly, still carefully averting her eyes from Spencer's. "We have a large inventory for you to choose from and we do all of the alterations here on site so you won't have to worry."

"So you work here as a model?" she asked.

"Just on Fridays," Penny replied and when Eva didn't comment, she figured she needed to clarify more. "During the week I'm an assistant manager of the dress shop and then I help out with our weekly fashion shows."

"That is so cool! It's like getting to play dress up all the time – like we used to when we were kids, remember?"

Just keep smiling, just keep smiling...

With a soft laugh, she said, "I do."

Crap. Had she really just said "I do" while wearing a wedding gown?

It was during one of those games of dress up that Spencer had first kissed her. She was six, he was eight and Eva had conned him into being the groom for their pretend wedding game. And ever since then, she'd been hooked.

On Spencer, not playing dress up.

"Hey, Penny." As if sensing her wayward thoughts, Spencer finally spoke.

Making sure she didn't show too much of a reaction, she turned to him and smiled. "Hey, Spencer. How are you?"

And damn. It was like a sucker punch to the gut just like it always was. He always had been her ideal man. Sandy brown hair, clear blue eyes and he still wore those wire-rimmed glasses that just totally worked for him.

She had to fight to keep herself from sighing dreamily.

"I'm fine," he said, smiling slowly. When it broadened, it brought out his dimples and Penny had to force her attention back to Eva.

"If you'd like, I can introduce you to the owners and they can set up an appointment for you to come in and try on gowns. There isn't a huge crowd tonight, so you might even be able to look at some now – if you have time, that is."

Eva let out a little squeal of delight. "We totally do! Right, Spence?" Then she looked at Penny again. "My poor brother drew the short straw tonight to come with me. He's only in town for a short time but no one else could come with me to the show so I convinced him it would be fun."

Spencer chuckled before adding, "She sweetened the deal by paying for dinner, so…"

Unable to help herself, Penny laughed with him. "You should definitely get the good brother award – especially if she starts shopping now."

Just then, one of Penny's other bosses walked over. "Hey, Hailey!" Penny said, getting her attention. "This is Eva and she is a bride with a short timeline. Any chance we have some time for her to look at our inventory tonight and then get an appointment?"

With the serene smile Hailey was known for, she introduced herself and replied, "Of course! Eva, why don't you come with me and we can talk about what you're looking for?"

And just like that, Penny was standing alone with Spencer.

While wearing a wedding gown.

And feeling kind of foolish about it.

"So…" he began.

"Um…yeah…so…"

"You look great," he said.

"It's the gown," she said, blushing.

But Spencer shook his head. "No. It's not the gown."

Damn. And just like that her knees were turning to jelly at his words. She was about to thank him when someone called her name. Looking over her shoulder, boss number three – Becca – was waving to her.

"I'm sorry but I need to go," she said quietly. "It looks like someone's interested in this gown."

The disappointment on his face was clear, but he didn't say anything. He merely tucked his hands into his pockets and nodded.

"It was good to see you, Spencer."

"You too."

And as she turned and walked away, Penny realized she didn't feel the relief quite like she thought she would.

Penny Blake.

Damn.

Spencer watched her walk away and wondered why he didn't stop her and at least ask for her number or if she'd like to get a cup of coffee sometime. Then he sighed. You'd think after knowing each other for twenty years and three breakups that this wouldn't be such a big deal.

But it was.

You didn't forget a girl like Penny.

Ever.

Looking around the massive showroom, he wondered what he was supposed to do with himself. He hadn't paid attention to where his sister had gone off to and now he felt a little foolish standing alone in the middle of the room. He walked toward the main door and then made his way toward the dress shop. If she was looking at gowns, that would be where she was, he imagined. He walked by a tuxedo shop, a flower shop, a photography studio, and a small coffee shop. Pausing, he looked around and realized that almost all of the shops were wedding-related.

Who knew there was even such a thing as a bridal mall?

Sure enough, he spotted his sister talking to Hailey in the bridal shop. She smiled when she spotted him and then looked at him curiously.

"What?" he asked. "What's the matter?"

"Where's Penny?"

He shrugged. "She had to get back to work, I guess. Someone called her over and she had to go."

Eva frowned a little. "Well damn."

"You know Penny?" Hailey asked. "I just thought you were asking her about her dress when I walked over." She was a very sophisticated looking woman – blonde hair done up in some sort of sleek style and dressed in a stylish suit.

"We do!" Eva said a little too enthusiastically. "We've been friends practically since kindergarten, but we'd lost track of each other years ago. I was so excited to see her here tonight." Then she smiled at Spencer. "Admit it, you were too."

What was he supposed to say to that? Especially here with an audience. There was the urge to roll his eyes at his sister's giddy tone, but he opted to reel it in. Luckily, he was spared from having to make a comment when Hailey spoke.

"Penny's amazing. She's my right-hand girl." Then she turned to Spencer. "We haven't been properly introduced. Hi, I'm Hailey."

He shook her hand. "Spencer Buchanan. Eva's brother."

Hailey smiled brightly. "Aren't you sweet for helping your sister out!"

He actually felt himself blush. "Yeah. That's me. Sweet," he said with a low chuckle.

"He's the best," Eva chimed in. "Seriously, I had no one to come with me tonight and Spencer took one for the team."

Hailey looked at her quizzically.

"Well, Brett can't come with me, now can he? And Mom is working the night shift at the hospital. Dad says he's writing the check for everything so that means he doesn't have to shop," she explained with a small laugh. Looking at Spencer, she smiled sweetly before adding, "That just left you."

"Somehow I doubt that. You probably had a ton of people to come with you. Bridesmaids or something," he replied. "You just wanted an excuse to torture me."

"That's just a perk," Eva said sassily before turning back to Hailey. "When is a good time to come in and try on gowns? And tuxes!" she quickly added. "The guys are going to need tuxes too!"

Spencer groaned. Wasn't it enough that he was here tonight? Why did this have to get dragged into more outings to the wedding mall?

"If you saw any tuxedos that you liked tonight at the show, I can write them down and when you're ready, we'll let the sales staff in the tux shop know and have them pulled for you."

"I didn't even think to look at them," Eva said with a pout. Then she looked at her brother. "Can you go and take a quick look, Spence? See if anyone's still walking around in the showroom? I totally trust your judgement."

The groan was louder this time. "Eva, I have

no idea what I'm supposed to be looking for," he protested. "And really, isn't this something Brett should be doing? After all, he is the groom."

"I know that, but if you help us get a head start, it would really save time. And you know you're going to be one of the groomsmen so go. Please? Please just go and look and maybe get some information? I'm going to be at least another fifteen minutes with Hailey," she went on. "Maybe flag down Penny and see if she can help you."

Ah. Now he realized what his sister was doing and he had to admit, he kind of approved.

Not that he was going to tell her that.

Instead he let out a sigh of agitation, looked at his watch and then glared at her. "You said this wasn't going to be an all-night thing."

Good, she clearly believed him because she looked a little crestfallen at his lack of enthusiasm.

He let out another sigh for good measure and then said, "Fine. But fifteen minutes, Eva." And as he turned and walked away he added, "And then you're going to owe me dessert!"

Even though his words sounded firm, he was grinning. With a little pep in his step, Spencer headed back to the showroom and at the entrance he quickly scanned the room. He spotted Penny easily enough – her long wavy red hair tended to stand out no matter what – and for a minute all he could do was take in how beautiful she was.

Still.

They had often joked that when he'd kissed her as her pretend groom when she was six that they had sealed their fate.

And right now, he kind of believed it.

Because all he wanted to do was walk over to her in her wedding gown, kiss her and make her his. For good this time.

Whoa…that was a big decision to make after only seeing her again for three minutes!

"Can I help you with something?"

Spencer blinked and looked at the woman standing in front of him. She was the same one Penny had been talking to earlier when he and Eva approached her.

"Um…my sister sent me back in here to look at tuxes but…"

She smiled. "You have no idea what you're supposed to look for, right?"

He nodded.

"I'm Angie," she said with a smile. She was tall and had a mass of dark curly hair and a southern twang. He had a feeling she'd be able to not only help him find a tux, but kick his ass if he got out of line. She just had that sort of presence about her.

Intimidating.

"Spencer," he replied. "It looks like a lot of the models have already cleared out so…"

"Hang on. There are still a few and maybe I can flag down one of the guys to help you." She looked around the room and then said, "Follow me."

It didn't take long for him to realize they were heading toward Penny and he said a silent prayer of thanks for whatever luck happened to be on his side tonight.

"Penny," Angie said when they got closer,

"Spencer needs help looking at some tuxes. I think Martin's gone home already because he has a sick kid. You've done some temping for them. Any chance you could help him out?"

It was funny how Spencer could almost hear what Penny was thinking – how this was definitely *not* something she wanted to do. At all. But her smile never fell. He had to hand her that. But right now, he was kind of thankful that she was being put on the spot and didn't seem to be able to say no.

"Um…sure. No problem," she said pleasantly. Then she looked at Spencer. "Does Eva know what she's looking for?"

"Not at all," he said with a small laugh. "I think she just wanted time to look at dresses without me hovering and looking at my watch."

"Have a good night," Angie said with a grin and a wave as she walked away.

There was a bit of an awkward moment as they both just looked at each other and if it were up to him, he'd keep looking at those blue eyes all night.

"So…um…" he began and then realized he had no idea what else he was going to say. They stood there in awkward silence for a long moment.

"Tuxes," Penny finally blurted out. "Um…" Then she looked down at herself and shook her head. "Kind of wish I wasn't still walking around in this."

Rather than agree or disagree, he held out his arm to her and said, "Come on. I may be dressed casually, but I think I can help you maneuver around like any of these guys in their fancy suits," he teased.

"That wasn't quite what I meant."

But he held out his arm to her in a dramatic fashion, while giving her – what he hoped – was a dashing smile. He felt a little chivalrous and was pleased when she hooked her arm through his.

"You're crazy," she said softly, but she *was* laughing. It was a great sound. And for the next few minutes, they walked around the showroom while she pointed out different tuxedo styles and designers.

Honestly, he was only half-listening to the information. He had no idea there were so many options and none of it really appealed to him – he was more focused on the sound of her voice and the feel of her arm in his. It was nice. Familiar.

And yet a little new and exciting.

"Your future brother-in-law should come in and take a look at them himself but really, unless he's looking for something extremely specific, any of these could work. Tell him the most important bit of information he'll need to know is the time of day for the wedding."

He stopped walking and looked at her. "That's the most important piece of information?"

She nodded.

"Why?"

"There are different styles of suits and tuxes for different times of day. Plus, we'll need to know how formal or casual the wedding will be."

"Ah…so there's really two important details you'll need," he teased again and smiled when she blushed. He was leaning in a little bit closer and could smell her perfume. It was a sweet scent with a hint of vanilla – just like he remembered.

Penny pulled back slightly and cleared her throat. "Um…yes. Yes, those two are really key in helping a groom pick out what he wants."

They were at a standstill – literally – and when she slowly pulled her arm from his, he knew she was getting ready to leave. "So…"

"So…" she said at the same time and then laughed.

"Listen, I'm only here visiting for a few days with my folks, but I'd love to take you out for coffee or…something," he said lamely. "Can we do that?"

When she didn't answer right away and seemed to glance away, he knew she was trying to come up with an excuse to say no.

"It's just coffee, right?" he asked quickly, nervously. "I'd just really like to sit and talk with you and catch up on what's been going on in your life."

"I don't know, Spencer…"

"Maybe we can…"

"There you are!" Great. Eva was back. They both turned toward her and he immediately noticed the excited look on his sister's face. "Oh good! You found her!" She practically skipped over.

Penny turned to him. "Oh…um…actually Angie – one of my bosses – asked me to help him look at some tuxes."

Eva looked at Spencer and he saw a hint of annoyance in her eyes, but she quickly masked it. "So? Did you find anything we can tell Brett about? Any great looking tuxes?"

When he stammered and hesitated, Penny spoke up and shared the information she told Spencer earlier. "Tell Brett to call Martin at the tuxedo shop. Tell Martin I sent him and he'll hook him up."

Eva beamed. "Perfect! Thank you!" Then she looked at Spencer. "I know you asked for dessert, but I'm kind of psyched to get home and call Brett to tell him about all of this. Why don't you and Penny go grab something? I'm sure you have a lot to catch up on!"

Smooth, he inwardly groaned. *Real smooth.* Could his sister be any more obvious?

Then he did something he wasn't too proud of, but…desperate times called for desperate measures.

"I actually had just asked Penny to join me for coffee when you interrupted us," he said smoothly and hoped his sister – who could be like a steamroller if you gave her a chance – would help convince Penny to accept his offer.

"You had?" Eva said excitedly. "That's great!" She looked at Penny with her biggest and brightest smile as she took one of Penny's hands in her own. "I can't thank you enough for all your help tonight! I had a great talk with Hailey and set up an appointment with her for early next week!"

"That's great, Eva. I know we'll be able to find your perfect dress."

The look on his sister's face was of pure happiness. "Well, besides the great help with the dress and hooking me up directly with Hailey, you also helped me get out of dessert with Spencer!" Then she laughed. "Not that I didn't want to have

15

dessert – I totally did! – but I'm just so excited to fill Brett in on all the details so we can keep moving forward with our plans. There is so much to do to plan a wedding on such short notice - I had no idea! And if I don't leave and do it now and get him on the same page, I fear we'll lose momentum!"

He wondered if she had even stopped to breathe during that speech…

Before he knew it, Eva was hugging Penny hard while making her promise they could get together for lunch soon. Then she turned and hugged him while murmuring something about not messing this up before practically skipping toward the door. "Have fun you two!"

The room was noticeably emptier and all of the models were gone. They both looked around and Spencer couldn't help but notice how it was only the cleaning crew milling around before he looked back at Penny. He couldn't help the nervous laugh that escaped. You'd think by now, at his age, he would be beyond this kind of thing. The nerves. And this was Penny. They'd known each other for so long and shared so much, how could he possibly be nervous?

Oh yeah, because you've broken her heart a time or two, or…three.

"So…coffee?"

"You have three minutes to give me the story of that sexy guy before I have to run," Angie said as she began to help Penny out of the wedding gown.

And if there was one thing she knew about this particular boss, it was that she was persistent. She wasn't going to let up until Penny told her what she wanted to know.

"I've known Spencer and Eva since I was five. We were neighbors. Eva and I would play dress up every day after school and we went through a wedding phase. Spencer was the first boy I ever kissed," she said and couldn't help but smile because to this day she could still remember that day so clearly. "I was six, he was eight."

"Okay, that is adorable…"

"We were pretending to get married and Eva demanded that we kiss and make it like a real wedding."

"Aww…"

"I know, right? I already had a bit of a crush on him, so it was perfect."

"Loving where this is going…"

"Then he made a face and told me that kissing me was gross and I better not tell anyone that he did it."

Angie laughed. "And that just ruined all the adorableness…"

"Talk about a mood-breaker, right?"

"I hope you slugged him."

She shook her head. "Nah. I moved on and after that, Eva and I decided that playing wedding dress-up wasn't our thing anymore and we moved on to being princesses."

"I remember my princess phase…" Angie said with a happy sigh. "So, then what?"

"He asked me out when I was in the sixth grade

and we dated for all of three months."

"At that age, that's practically a lifetime," Angie commented.

Penny nodded. "It was. But we were young, and the age difference was kind of an issue. We didn't have a lot in common – he was into academic clubs and activities and I wasn't. He's really smart – like crazy super smart," she explained. "And I was just really immature. That's what he told me at the time – I was a little too immature for him."

"Well that's sucky."

She nodded again. "I know, but accurate."

"So then what happened?"

"His dad got a new job – he was an architect – and it was a big deal. Big promotion for him. And they moved across town to a new house – a really big one in a very swanky neighborhood. Eva and I didn't get to hang out as much and she started making new friends and…"

"You guys started drifting."

"Yup." Then she shrugged and stepped out of the gown and turned to help get it back on its hanger. Standing in her underwear, she continued the story. "The summer between ninth and tenth grade, Eva invited me over for a sleepover and of course, Spencer was there."

"So he was getting ready for his senior year?"

Nodding, Penny zipped up the garment bag and turned to grab her jeans. "I spent most of the night talking to him instead of Eva – but that was because she was on the phone with her boyfriend," she clarified. "Anyway, we talked and laughed, and I was still crushing so damn hard on him that when he kissed me, I was speechless."

"A good kiss should leave you that way."

"I agree, and it did," she said with a sigh. "We dated that entire summer and I thought things were great but...I guess they weren't. When school started we realized – again – how different we were and it just wasn't working." She slid her sweater on and then sat down on the dressing room bench to pull on her boots.

"You were in high school," Angie commented. "What wasn't working?"

"He was dealing with college applications and he was still involved in all of the academic and business clubs and by that point I was a cheerleader. He saw what I was doing as pointless and I saw what he was doing as boring."

"Ah...I can see that being a problem. Total opposites."

"It was and...we fought about it. He called me superficial and I called him...hell, something about him being boring and having no friends," she said with disgust. The words were a blur, but she still remembered how much she had wanted to hurt him with them.

And she had.

And it didn't feel nearly as good as she thought it would.

"Is this the first time you're seeing him since then?" Angie asked, her eyes a little wide.

Standing up, Penny checked her reflection in the mirror and picked up her purse. "We saw each other at Eva's graduation party, but other than that...yeah. This is the first time I'm seeing him."

"Did you talk to him at the graduation party?"

"Um…yeah. I mean…sort of." Her cheeks felt like they were on fire and she couldn't bring herself to actually meet Angie's gaze.

"Oh my God! Did you hook up with him at the graduation party?" Angie cried out and then quickly covered her mouth. "Sorry." Then she repeated her question in a much lower tone.

Blushing, Penny moved in close and whispered, "Let's just say we…did a little more than just talk."

And oh boy had they, she remembered.

Spencer Buchanan was the one who got away. They just weren't meant to be. And even as her cheeks continued to heat at the memory of what they had done that one night, Penny always regretted that it wasn't enough to keep them together.

Or even keep in touch.

Yeah. That part had been a little awkward. Spencer had asked for her number, but she was getting ready to go off to college and didn't see a point to taking things beyond…well, beyond. Seeing him now reminded her of just how much she wished she'd handled things differently. All the things. Every time.

"So what are you going to do now?" Angie asked as they stepped out of the dressing room. She was carrying the wedding gown and when Penny offered to put it away, she waved her off.

"It looks like I'm going to go and have coffee with him – thanks to Eva," she murmured. If she didn't know any better, Penny would think that the two of them had set her up. Eva had always said how she hated that Penny and Spencer couldn't seem to get it together, but that was years ago. She needed to forget about the past and focus on the present.

The here and now.

After wishing Angie a good night, Penny gave herself a quick mental pep talk – *It's just coffee. And no matter what, do not give Spencer Buchanan the opportunity to break your heart again. You're a good person with a lot to offer. Be strong. Stay strong. Your time with him is in the past and you can't go back. Remember that.*

And when she stepped out of the bridal shop and found Spencer waiting for her by the main entrance, she knew she was lying to herself.

She was never going to be able to forget about the past where he was concerned. He was a major part of it. And after seeing him again – even if it was only for coffee – she knew he'd be playing a major part in her current fantasies.

And her future ones.

Dammit.

With a steadying breath, she walked toward him. "So…where to?"

"Is that diner still in business? The one over by First and Main?"

She nodded. They used to go to that one a lot during their summer together. It wasn't the closest one to their present location, but it was kind of nice that he remembered it. "Should I meet you there?"

"Oh…um…I thought you realized…"

Penny looked at him curiously.

"Eva was my ride so…"

It looked like not only was she having coffee with Spencer, but she was driving him home as well.

Then he smiled at her until those dimples appeared and it was official…

It didn't matter that it was just coffee. She wasn't sure her hormones would be able to stand it.

TWO

They drove and they talked about how much things had changed in Raleigh since they were younger and Spencer couldn't remember the last time he had felt so relaxed and carefree. He'd followed in his father's footsteps by becoming an architect and he was currently considering taking over the firm his father had started five years ago. Actually, considering wasn't quite the term he'd use – being pressured to take it over? That was a little more fitting.

Not that he was totally against it. It was just that his father had built something and it was all fine and well, but Spencer had bigger plans – plans his father wasn't on board with. So they were currently at a standstill. And for far too long, it was all he had been thinking about – weighing the pros and cons of it all – and there seemed to be way too many cons at this point. It was becoming a mild obsession since it was all his father wanted to talk about, turning their once-a-week phone call into a three-to-four time per week thing. It was so consuming that he hadn't had much time for anything else – certainly not a social life.

And definitely not dating.

He glanced over at Penny as she drove. She was chatting about the benefit to all of the new additions to the downtown area and pointed out the new Trader Joe's where there used to be a bowling alley.

"Did you ever think about moving away from here?" he blurted out.

"Not really," she replied and then gave him a small smile. "This is home. I love it here."

With a shrug, Spencer wasn't sure what to say to that. It wasn't that he didn't enjoy living in Raleigh – or anywhere in North Carolina per se – but he just felt like he wanted something different. Something that was his and his alone and…

"Plus, my whole family is still here – I mean, most of them," she continued.

Penny came from a large family. She was the youngest of nine kids. Spencer had to admit that he was more than a little surprised that she – more than anyone – wasn't more interested in getting away and having a life of her own that was separate from…well…what she had grown up with. Hell, it was just him and Eva growing up and that felt stifling. How did Penny stand it with that many siblings?

Thinking back, he realized that she never complained about it. Ever. Any time she had ever talked about her family, it was with a smile on her

face and there was always a funny story to tell.
When they were younger, he remembered looking
at the Blakes as an oddity, but maybe it was his own
family that was odd.

"How is your family? Who moved away?" he
asked.

A low laugh came out first and then she took a
breath before starting. "Okay, Steven and his wife
now have four kids and live in Charlotte. Patti and
her husband have three kids and are still here in
Raleigh and so is Debbie and her family – she's
pregnant with her third child. They have two boys
and are really hoping for a girl this time. Tina
recently got divorced and has two kids and they're
currently living back with my mom and dad." She
paused. "Mark is married. He and his wife have
one child and live up in Asheville. Kristen and Jill
are both married and each have twins of their own –
weird right? – and they're local too. And Laura and
her husband have two kids and they recently moved
to Baltimore." Letting out a breath, she glanced at
him and smiled. "Just don't ask me to name all the
nieces and nephews because I don't think I could do
it all and drive at the same time."

He laughed with her and when she pulled into
the diner's parking lot, he realized how much he
enjoyed talking with her. They never had a problem
with that – conversation always came naturally to
them – but it just hit him hard in that moment how
much time really had gone by since they'd seen
each other. Too much time, he thought.

Their last conversation was years ago and
Spencer knew that they had each gone on to live

their lives. But...what had she done in those years? Where had she traveled? What had she ended up studying at school? Was there something specific that led her to her job at the bridal mall? For years she had been on his mind more than she wasn't. If he had been braver – bolder – he would have reached out to her sooner. If nothing else, as a friend. All those years ago she had been so outgoing and confident, and he'd often wondered if she'd gone on to do great things.

But most of all, he had to wonder if she had ever thought about him.

Inwardly, he groaned. He was walking a slippery slope here. Maybe she had thought about him, but probably not too fondly. Spencer knew his strengths and weaknesses and Penny had a way of making him behave in ways that he never had with anyone else.

And it wasn't usually even remotely flattering.

Looking back, he knew he should have fought harder to get her number and keep in touch. God, how many times had he thought about her? Wondered where she was and what she was doing? How many times had he fought with himself about looking her up on social media and just saying hi?

But had he?

No.

Coward.

Yeah. That definitely seemed to be more of his M.O. where she was concerned; he knew if given the chance, he'd change it. All of it. Every unkind word, every flippant attitude...every time he let her walk away.

"You ready?" she asked, grabbing her purse and opening the car door.

Offering her a small smile, he replied, "Sure."

He fought the urge to take her by the hand and walk into the diner like they used to way back when. It felt weird and he was a little at a loss at how to act around her. They seemed to only have two speeds – together or apart. This in between that they were experiencing right now was brand new. Once they were seated and had ordered some dessert and coffee, Penny looked up at him and asked about his life. And being that she had just gotten the update on Eva, he knew she wasn't referring to family.

A weary sigh came out as he raked a hand through his hair. "I'm an architectural engineer and I'm with a firm down in Atlanta."

She cocked her head, her expression serious. "You don't sound happy about it."

Relaxing a bit, Spencer leaned forward and rested his arms on the table. "I actually love what I do," he began. "I've designed some great buildings, the work is challenging but I thrive under it."

"But…?"

"But lately I'm feeling the pressure to take over my father's firm." He gave her a half-hearted grin. "He started it up a little over five years ago after spending most of his life working for someone else. It's a perfectly fine firm – different from what I'm doing now – and…"

"And you don't want to do that," she stated.

"That's the thing. I'm not sure," he admitted. "At least, I think I'm not."

When Penny didn't comment, he clarified – for her and for himself. Talking out loud usually helped him when he had big decisions to make.

It was just that recently, he tended to be alone, talking to himself.

"What I do is very different from what he does. He's residential, I'm commercial. And that's not to say that I can't do residential design or don't want to – that's not it – but it's a completely different mindset. His firm is small and it's very successful but..." He shrugged.

"It's not what you want to do," she said softly.

How was it that she grasped in two minutes what he'd been arguing with his parents about for almost a year? "If I do what he's asking, I'm not sure either of us will be happy."

"How come?"

"Because he's not looking to change anything or see anything change, I should say. He wants me to step directly into his place and keep doing things his way." He looked at her helplessly. "I don't think I can do that. I feel like my creativity would be completely stifled."

Their waitress came back with their food and after they thanked her, they ate in companionable silence for a few minutes.

"What about if you came on as a partner?" she asked. "Maybe if you were coming in and expanding the business – making it a father and son operation – he'd see that not all change is bad. Your dad is still young to be retiring – unless...there's another reason why he's looking for you to take over."

Spencer shook his head. "I think he's just tired
and looking to cut back a little bit. Part of me is
afraid that he's not actually going to cut back and
then I'll have him hovering over my shoulder every
day and that will just make me crazy. You
remember how I couldn't wait to move away and be
on my own?" He sighed. "And I'm in a really
good place with the firm back home. I'm hoping to
make partner by the end of next year. At least,
that's the track I'm on and…"

"So you enjoy living in Atlanta?" she asked
and not at all in an accusatory way; she seemed
genuinely interested.

He nodded. "It's all right. Big city, tons of
stuff to do…what's not to like?"

Only…there were a lot of things he could think
of off the top of his head. None of them were the
fault of the location just…him. For all the things to
do, he never went anywhere. He didn't travel, he
didn't socialize much he just…worked. A lot. All
the time.

Why was this all just coming to him now?

When he sighed again and pushed his plate
away, Penny asked, "Are you okay? Do you not
like the pie?"

He was eating a slice of apple pie and it was
fine but…even that wasn't right at the moment.
Shit. When did he become so discontent with
everything? Pushing his coffee cup aside as well,
he felt bold. He reached across the table and took
one of her hands in his and noticed her soft gasp as
her eyes met his.

"I'm sitting here with you and it's all just

29

hitting me that I'm not okay," he admitted. "When we were driving here, I was thinking how much fun I was having and how I couldn't remember the last time I had had any. I love our conversations and I can't remember the last time I had one that didn't revolve around a building." He squeezed her hand slightly. "My whole life I thought I knew what I wanted and now…? I just don't know." Then he looked at her. "But when I'm with you…things just seem better. Clearer. Does that make sense?"

"Spencer…"

"No, it's true," he quickly interrupted, unwilling to let her try to tell him he was wrong, or worse, crazy. "I feel like there isn't anything I can't say to you that you wouldn't understand. You're probably one of the only people who's ever been able to do that. I've missed that about us. I…I miss *you*."

For a moment, neither of them spoke and Spencer wasn't sure if that was a good thing or a bad thing. All he knew was that it felt good to say those things out loud to her.

"Spencer," she began and then slowly pulled her hand from his. "This is…this is what always happens with us. We see each other and we always have great conversations and a lot of fun until…we don't."

Her tone was just a little sad and it bothered him more than he thought it could.

"For whatever reason, we keep coming back to each other and think it's a good thing – that it will be better, different. But it doesn't take long for one of us – *me* – to suddenly not measure up to whatever it is in your mind." She gently pushed her plate away and gingerly wiped at her mouth with her napkin.

"That's not true…"

Then even her smile turned sad. "It is." She paused and seemed to carefully consider her next words. "In the past you've accused me of being immature, superficial and even a bad kisser…"

"I was eight and I had no idea what I was talking about!" he argued lightly, but when he reached for her hand again, she moved it away.

Not a good sign.

"I'll give you a pass on that one, but the point still remains…" She sighed. "Look at me, Spencer. This is who I am."

"I am looking at you. Hell, I haven't been able to take my eyes off of you," he admitted.

"You're attracted to this…this outer image," she said softly. "That's it. I'm never going to be some crazy smart intellectual person. I'm never going to have some high-powered career and you know what? I'm really okay with that! I refuse to feel bad because I didn't go to an Ivy League school or wasn't the valedictorian in high school."

"I never said that…"

"I'm working at Enchanted and I have my glam squad business plan and I'm happy! And I learned a long time ago not to let someone else's closed-mindedness take that joy from me. I can't." Then she paused. "I wish you'd do the same."

"What do you mean?"

"What makes you happy, Spencer? What brings you joy? What has *ever* brought you joy?"

31

You.

But he didn't say it. What would be the point? Right now, she wasn't ready to hear that and if he was being honest, he wasn't sure he was ready to say it out loud.

No matter how comfortable she made him feel.

When the waitress came by and asked if they wanted anything else, Penny asked for the check and he didn't bother to correct her. It was getting late and his mind was spinning in a dozen different directions. It would probably be a good thing to go back to his parents' house and spend some time alone to think.

And man did he suddenly have a lot think about.

Then something Penny had said earlier came to him.

"What's a glam squad business plan?"

"Oh…um…glam squad is kind of my thing. I do hair and makeup – I'm a certified cosmetologist – and I not only help with that for the fashion shows, but it's a service I provide for bridal parties too."

"I don't remember you talking about going to school for that back when you and Eva graduated."

She shrugged. "I went to UNC Wilmington for business and found that I was bored. I didn't overly enjoy college life – dorm life, actually. It felt an awful lot like I was still living at home because I had to share a bathroom with so many people." Laughing softly, she moved her napkin around idly. "So, I talked to my folks about coming home and taking some business courses at the community college and they agreed."

"And when did you realize you wanted to go into cosmetology?" he asked, finding he was mildly fascinated to be learning this about her.

The expression on her face was like a silent reprimand. "I've always wanted to do that, Spencer," she said quietly. "I just never told you."

"But…why? I think it's kind of cool."

Another bland look from her put him in his place. "Again, after having you call me superficial, I didn't particularly want to talk to you about going to beauty school."

"Penny…"

"No, I'm serious! How do you think you would have reacted back then?" Now there was a little heat behind her words. "You would have made a comment on how that was a typical career choice for someone like me – someone who only cared about appearances." Then she stopped and seemed to will herself to calm down.

"I had no idea," he began. "I didn't realize I made you feel that way."

It took her a minute, but she sat up a little straighter and looked him in the eye. "I'm proud of the work I do. And if all goes as planned, this time next year I'll have my own little spot at Enchanted Bridal," she stated proudly.

"Really? Good for you! That's impressive!"

"Thank you for saying that. I know it's not much but…it's something I've wanted to do for a long time." She paused and shrugged. "The whole thing overwhelms me. I always thought I would eventually have a shop of my own someplace, but the thought of being in with Enchanted was an amazing opportunity. This way I can build the business while still working for Hailey part-time at the bridal shop."

"Will you really need to still work for her?"

"In the beginning I will, I'm sure. Hopefully it will only be temporary. The upside is that I love what I do with the bridal shop. Staying on there won't be a hardship."

Studying her for a moment, he realized what she'd said. "Why don't you think it's much? You're looking to start your own business. That's always a big thing!"

She gave him a bland look. "Oh, I know it's a big thing, but compared to what you do...you know...I just figured you might not see it that way."

And he felt like the biggest jerk in the world. Had he really been that much of a snob back then? So much so that this was the memory – the impression - she had of him?

He shook his head and felt his dessert turn in his stomach. "Penny...I am so sorry if I ever made you feel like you weren't good enough. Hell, who am I to say that about you or anyone? I think what you're doing is amazing."

"You do?" she asked, but Spencer could hear the skepticism in her voice.

"Hell yes I do!" And this time when he reached for her hand, she didn't pull it away. "I think your decision to be a part of Enchanted is very smart. You'll have a customer base that's already established and then you'll get to build on that. And because I know you, I know you're going to make a success of it. Earlier, Hailey was saying you're her right-hand girl. It's obvious she thinks highly of you and no doubt she'll support you with this endeavor."

She blushed and it was sweet and sexy all at the same time.

Their check was placed on the table and Spencer immediately picked it up. Penny started to argue but he simply held up a hand to stop her. "I asked you out for coffee, didn't I?"

She didn't comment. Instead, she grabbed her purse and left the tip.

Stubborn woman.

As they stood in the lobby and looked out at the parking lot, Spencer sighed. Tonight was certainly a night of revelations and maybe he should just say goodnight here.

"I hate putting you out and asking you to drive me home," he began cautiously. "I can just grab an Uber home."

For a minute all Penny did was study him. "It's not really a big deal. I don't mind driving you home."

"You're sure?"

"Positive." He wasn't sure what to do or say and after a few silent moments, they agreed they should go. They were back in Penny's car now, but with Spencer behind the wheel. It was starting to rain and his parents had moved since she had last seen them so he figured it would just be easier for him to drive.

The conversation went back to nostalgia as they drove by more familiar landmarks and some newer ones and he cursed the fact that they were pulling into his parents' driveway so soon. There was a loud crack of thunder and a flash of lightning and now he worried about her driving home.

"I hope your drive isn't very far," he said. "I had no idea it was supposed to storm tonight."

"Me either," she replied. "But…it will be okay." Pausing, she added, "But it is getting late and it's been a long day so…"

It didn't seem fair. He didn't want the night to end and if he wasn't staying at his parents' house, he would invite her in. "You're sure you're okay driving in this? It's really coming down now."

It was pouring.

Damn near monsooning.

"I'll be fine," she said softly.

"Can I call you?" he asked tentatively.

Penny didn't quite look at him. "I don't think that's a good idea. It was really good to see you, Spencer but…"

She didn't finish, and he didn't push.

"Well…I guess…um…be careful driving home."

"Thanks."

Penny opted to get out of the car and come around to the driver's side rather than climb over the console of the small SUV. She ran around as Spencer held the door open for her. But rather than climbing in right away, she stopped right in front of him. In just those few seconds, they were both already soaked from the rain.

And still he couldn't move.

They were standing close together and there

wasn't anything else to do or say. She needed to get in her car and warm up and Spencer needed to…well, he just needed to leave and take this for what it was – a chance meeting at the wrong place and at the wrong time in his life.

Again.

"Spencer, I…"

Screw it. He'd kick himself years from now if he didn't take a chance – if he didn't at least try.

Reaching up, he cupped his hand around her nape as he leaned down and kissed her.

It was quite possibly the most exciting moment of her life. Standing in the pouring rain and kissing Spencer Buchanan.

Finally kissing Spencer Buchanan.

And it was even better than she remembered.

His lips were soft and demanding all at the same time. He didn't just kiss; he took, he devoured, he claimed. And Penny was completely on board with that. Her hands reached up and gripped the front of his shirt to pull him closer. It was completely crazy. She rubbed up against him even as his arms banded around her to hold her and all she wanted to do was climb him and wrap her legs around him. Hell, if she could, she'd pull him right into the car and wrap her entire body around him!

She opened one eye and considered opening the back door and getting them both out of the rain. But just as she was about to suggest it, Spencer broke the kiss. Both of their breathing was ragged, and he slowly trailed one rough finger along her cheek before he took a step back.

"Good night, Penny," he said gruffly.

She called after him, but there was a boom of thunder that shook her to her bones and several flashes of lightning that swallowed the sound of her voice. By the time things were quiet again, Spencer was standing in the doorway of his parents' massive home. She knew he would continue to stand there and watch and wait until she was back in her car. It took her a solid minute to get her head clear enough to register that she was soaked to the skin and then she gave him a weak wave before climbing in and shutting the door.

She instantly turned on the heat and took a minute to try to warm herself up. Lights came on along the driveway and the front of the house and still Spencer stood and watched her.

She had to give him points for being a gentleman, at least.

And a great kisser.

And still holding the top spot of the perfect man and star of all her fantasies.

Dammit.

So now what? What was she supposed to do? Was she supposed to just forget about that amazing kiss or was she supposed to find an excuse to get out of the car and go and talk to him? Or maybe she needed to wait and do that in a day or two? Was it foolish not to give him her phone number?

She had no idea.

And unfortunately, she knew she was going to

obsess about it until she made herself crazy.

With nothing left to do, she offered another small wave before pulling out of the driveway. The entire drive home was spent alternating between smacking herself in the head for being so stubborn and high-fiving herself for sticking to her guns and not giving Spencer the chance to hurt her again.

There was too much history there – too many past hurts to overcome. She was at a place in her life where she finally felt like she was getting her shit together – being responsible and making plans for her future. No doubt if she gave Spencer the chance to come back into her life, he'd undo all of the hard work she'd put into building her self-esteem and becoming the confident woman she was today. Why would she jeopardize all of that when she already knew how it was going to end?

Only…she had a feeling it wouldn't be quite like that this time around. They were older, more mature and…

"Stop it," she snapped at herself. She spent the rest of the drive singing to the radio to distract herself and fifteen minutes later, she pulled up to her condo. It was a rental and it was small, but it was home. Right now, she couldn't wait to get inside and get out of her wet clothes and just…be. And with that thought in mind, she climbed from the car and made a mad dash to her door and then quickly slipped inside, bolting the door behind her.

"It's good to be home," she sighed.

But…was it? The warmth was great and knowing she was minutes away from being dry was even better but…she was alone. There was no one here to greet her and normally that didn't bother her. Tonight, however, it did.

A lot.

And dammit if Spencer Buchanan hadn't done it to her again.

✍✍

For the next week, Penny agonized over what she should do and then realized that it didn't matter. Spencer had mentioned that he was only in town for a short time so he was probably back in Atlanta by now. He lived there, had a life there, and from the things they talked about over dessert, he didn't seem too anxious to move back to Raleigh.

And a long-distance relationship was not something she wanted to even consider.

They had enough trouble in the past with being together. Why add the extra stress of living two states away into the mix?

It's better this way, she thought. And no matter how many times her brain tried to tell her otherwise, she simply kept reminding herself of that.

Over and over.

More times than she should have.

Why? Why couldn't she just let this go and chalk it up to a moment of weakness? That's exactly how she reasoned her giving in and kissing Spencer.

Weakness.

That was all. Nothing more, nothing less.

Maybe they should look at it as finally getting some closure. Okay, maybe she needed to look at it that way. She had no idea what Spencer was thinking.

But it still didn't answer the question why – why was she still thinking about him?

Because you have no social life, no dating prospects – even within the state.

Oh, right. That.

Fine, so right now she wasn't dating anyone. That wasn't a big deal. It wasn't for lack of trying, but her schedule just wasn't conducive to having a relationship. She worked weekends and three out of four Friday nights a month were spent doing the fashion show, so really, when most couples were out on dates, Penny wasn't available.

It had only taken three failed relationships for her to figure out that her job was the problem.

Not that it had deterred her. She loved what she did and knew there would eventually come a time when her hours would change. In the meantime, she would be patient.

And she had been until Spencer showed up.

Now she wanted…something. That one kiss had reminded her how she missed being in a relationship, missed the comfort of being held by a man, kissed by a man, desired by a man.

"Ugh…" she groaned, doing her best to try and focus on other things.

So she worked at Enchanted during the day and worked on her business plan at night because really, she had neglected it for too long. That was one thing she should be thankful to Spencer for – he had given her that little nudge she needed to get herself moving. Every night she looked over her plan and her sketches for what she wanted her space to look like before going over her ideas for logos and web designs. It was all overwhelming and yet she knew if she could take that last step and do the presentation in front of Hailey, Becca, Angie, and Ella she'd be okay.

They were a lot less intimidating than the bank and she knew they'd be the ones to really make her take that final step.

It was Friday night and the one Friday a month when they didn't hold a fashion show. Penny couldn't contain the sigh of relief that came out at the thought of there not being a show. She loved them; she really did, but they were a lot of work and she was looking forward to getting out of work by eight and having the weekend off.

Yeah, it was her weekend off and she had zero plans.

Other than laundry.

This so wasn't how she imagined her life being.

She was working on pulling gowns for tomorrow's bride appointments when Hailey approached her.

"Hey, you got a minute?"

Nodding, Penny put the dress she was holding back on the rack. "Sure. What's up?"

"I know it's seven-thirty and almost time for you to leave, but I have a favor to ask," Hailey said, and it was clear she was hesitant to go on. That normally meant that she wasn't going to get her weekend off and she mentally braced herself for the news.

"O-kay…"

"Martin had to leave because his daughter caught what his son had last week, his wife is ready to lose her mind, and he got a last-minute call about a groomsman coming in for a fitting. I'm swamped here with paperwork and Angie's already gone and…would you mind going down to the tuxedo shop and manning the desk and helping the groomsman out? It's just the one guy and Martin's already pulled the tuxes so it's really just a matter of you standing there and taking his info. What do you think?"

Relief almost had her weeping with gratitude. Her weekend was safe! Again, not that she had any plans, but she was looking forward to the down time. "Not a problem. Any idea what time he's due to arrive?"

"Martin said any minute. He tried to get the guy to reschedule but apparently this was the only time he was available to come in."

"It's no big deal. Really. If it's all right with you, I'll grab my purse and jacket and run down there."

"You are a lifesaver, Penny. Thank you." She handed her the spare set of keys so she could lock up when she was done and praised her as she walked away.

Five minutes later, she was putting her purse behind the desk at the tuxedo shop and hoping this groomsman wouldn't keep her waiting too long.

Off in the distance she heard the main doors in the lobby open and close followed by voices calling out a greeting. She looked over at the rack by the fitting rooms and saw that Martin had indeed already pulled a couple of tuxedoes and with any luck, she wouldn't be out of here much later than her usual time.

Chinese takeout was calling her name and she couldn't wait to curl up in her yoga pants and a sweatshirt while she enjoyed some dumplings and maybe binge-watched something on Netflix.

She looked toward the front of the shop because if that had been her groomsman walking in the lobby, he would have been in here by now. With a shrug, she decided to get a jump on her dining plans. Bending down, she quickly reached into her purse and pulled out her phone. And when she straightened, she found herself face to face with Spencer.

∾⌇∾

For a minute, he thought she was going to scream and the expression on her face said that she certainly hadn't been expecting him. Actually, he hadn't been expecting her either. His plan had been to come in for a tuxedo fitting – something he was seriously jumping the gun for Eva's wedding – and figured it would be a legit excuse to see Penny. He'd casually stop in at the bridal shop and say hello and then…

"Spencer? What are you doing here?"

He gave her a lopsided grin. "Doing a test run on tuxedoes to help Eva and Brett out."

At first he didn't think she believed him, but then she visibly relaxed. "Oh. Okay."

"So what are you doing in the tuxedo shop? I

didn't think you worked in here too."

She quickly explained about the owner needing to get home to a sick child – again – and then she stepped away and began to explain to him about the tuxedo options that had been pulled for him.

If he didn't know any better, he'd swear she was nervous and that pleased him a little. If she was nervous around him, that meant that she wasn't unaffected by him – or by their kiss.

Good to know.

Because kissing Penny had been all he could think about all week. He should be back in Atlanta right now.

But he wasn't.

He should be working on reports for the building he was designing.

But he wasn't.

What he *was* doing was trying on tuxedoes when he didn't need to just on the off-chance he could see her again. How twisted was that?

By now Penny was standing next to a dressing room and holding a tuxedo hanger in her hand. "Martin already placed a shirt and shoes in the fitting room for you," she said, "and this is the first tux he pulled for you to consider based on your measurements."

"I never gave him my measurements," Spencer said.

"Um…what?"

He nodded. "All I did was call and ask if I could come in and try some on," he explained. "No one asked for any sizes or measurements. I guess I can try this on and we can go from there, right?"

Then he watched as her shoulders sagged and she sighed. But she immediately went back into sales mode and gave him a nice but professional smile. "Okay, we'll need to get your measurements first. No need for you to try to fit into a suit that isn't your size. That's just crazy." She stepped away and hung up the suit she had in her hands. "Why don't you step up on the platform over there by the mirror and I'll go get the measuring tape."

Wait…measuring tape? Couldn't he just tell her what size he normally wore? That would certainly make things easier – especially since Brett hadn't made any decisions on tuxedos and he wasn't planning on ordering anything tonight. Then again, if he did happen to go in that direction, there'd be no need for him to stand up on the platform for measurements. And that would mean…

"Just step up on there and face the mirror," she said. "I'll need to make a note of your shirt and sleeve size, waist, outseam…"

Then he felt bad for giving her extra work. "Wouldn't it be easier to give you at least some of my sizes so you don't have to go through all of this?" he asked and hated that he was quite possibly depriving himself of some extra time with her.

"Under normal circumstances, yes," she explained. "But for this sort of thing, we require specific measurements. Every designer is cut just a litter differently so it makes everyone's job easier to just go by what the measuring tape says."

"Ah…gotcha." Doing his best to hide a grin, he simply stood and did as he was told as Penny's hands roamed all over him – in a completely professional way – as she took the needed measurements.

Best. Friday. Night. Ever.

At first, he felt all kinds of wrong that even though there was nothing sexy about what she was doing, it was still mildly arousing – her hand skimming down his leg…her arms wrapped around him to get his waist measurements…

He cursed the fact that they were in the middle of a tuxedo shop and that he had on so many damn clothes!

Once she was done, she moved around the shop and pulled tuxes in his size and then sent him back to the dressing room to start trying them on.

They didn't talk about much – she kept all of the conversation focused on Eva and Brett and their wedding and tuxedo style questions. Not that he cared. Basically, this was all going to be Brett's decision and right now, Brett had no idea that Spencer was even looking at tuxes.

No one did.

If his sister caught wind of what he was doing, he knew he'd get her approval and possibly her help. And as much as he knew he was going to need some of that where Penny was concerned, he wanted to do it in his own time and in his own way.

He just never thought trying on tuxedos was a length he'd ever have to go through in order to spend time with a woman.

"Let me know how that first one fits," Penny called out to him.

And as he closed the dressing room door, he

figured he had at least an hour to try to break down some of her defenses and convince her to go out with him again.

THREE

It was one thing to fantasize about touching Spencer.

It was quite another to actually be doing it.

I love my job.

"How does the jacket feel?" she forced herself to ask as she continued to smooth imaginary wrinkles. "Is it too tight? Too loose? Can you move comfortably?"

Spencer's expression was serious as he took in his reflection. Stepping back, she let him move his arms and shoulders to get the feel of the suit jacket. It looked good on him. Really good on him. But then again, Penny had a feeling that anything would look good on him. He was tall and lean, she noticed, with just the right amount of muscle – he'd filled out in all the best ways in the last ten years. And as much as she hated to admit it, he was just…

Perfect, she inwardly sighed.

"It feels all right," he said, his voice deep and

just a little gruff. "Can we try the next size up? I think it's just a little snug in the shoulders."

"No problem," she replied softly as she went to pull another jacket from the rack. After taking all of his measurements – neck, sleeve, waist, outseam, and shoulders – she had been fairly confident that she picked the right size for him. But if he wasn't one-hundred percent comfortable, who was she to argue?

Stepping over to him, she helped him remove the jacket he had on before handing him the new one. He was mesmerizing to watch. Some guys could come in and try on jackets and it would register zero on her radar, but watching Spencer Buchanan try on a jacket was borderline porn for her right now.

Quickly, she turned away, hung up the jacket and placed it to the side in case he wanted it back for comparison. She seriously needed to compose herself before going any further. If she could, she would have stepped outside to fan herself or grab something cold to drink because it suddenly felt very warm in the shop.

Pull yourself together!

Stepping back up on the platform with him, she began her tasks of smoothing and gently tugging and adjusting and helping him get the true feel of the garment. She wanted to smack herself because she knew she was being a little excessive in the touching department but…she couldn't seem to help herself.

"How about this one?" she asked, smiling at him in the mirror and hoping he didn't hear the slight tremor in her voice. "Is this one more comfortable?"

"This one definitely feels more comfortable," he said, interrupting her thoughts. "I'm not crazy about these trousers, though."

Her heart kicked a little and she felt a slight flutter in her belly at those words. It was one thing to be able to touch his back, his arms, his shoulders…but to be kneeling down and running her hands over his legs and waist? Well…it had been a little awkward when she was measuring him a few minutes ago and she wasn't sure she'd survive it a second time.

Clearing her throat, she forced herself to focus. "All of your measurements will go to our warehouse and everything will be custom-tailored for you. The inventory we have here is just the basics, so they won't necessarily fit you like this."

He nodded but didn't really look at her; he was still studying his reflection. "I think the measurements on the outseam weren't quite right. I'd like to try a pair of different shoes and then measure again if that's all right with you."

Um…yes please, she thought and immediately wanted to smack herself. Honestly, she had no idea if any of this was the norm for getting a tuxedo fitting – she'd never had to do quite so much before, but right now she couldn't find the will to stop any of it.

"No problem," Penny replied. "Would you like to go pick out another pair?"

For a few minutes, Spencer walked around and tried on shoes while Penny made notes in his file.

When he stepped back onto the platform, she was ready with her measuring tape. Standing to his left, she carefully kneeled – not an easy feat in her navy pencil skirt and heels. Doing her best to stay balanced, she carefully measured the outseam with minimal amounts of running her hand along his muscled calf. Standing slowly, she went and did the same on the right.

This time when she went to stand, Spencer stopped her.

"Isn't it customary to measure the inseam as well?"

Oh. Right. The inseam.

"Um...yes. Yes. You're right. Sorry about that," she nervously stammered. "I'm not fully familiar with all the procedures." With a steadying breath, she moved until she was in front of him. "Can you...um...just widen your stance a little?"

His gaze was a little intense as he looked down at her. Doing as she requested, he asked, "Like this?"

Was it wrong that she could barely remember how to speak because she was eye level with...well...what was a rather *impressive* part of him?

"That's fine," she murmured and did her best to hold the tape measure at the top of his inseam as she ran her other hand down his leg. By the time she got that measurement and did his other leg, she was practically sweating.

Mentally, she was about to congratulate herself on doing the job without embarrassing herself, but as she went to straighten, she lost her balance and cried out as she felt herself about to fall. "Oh!"

Spencer quickly swooped down and banded an arm around her waist to catch her and pulled her to her feet. Chest to chest, her heart racing, Penny looked up at him and knew she was blushing.

"You okay?" he asked, a small smile tugging at his lips.

She couldn't speak. Up close, he was even more handsome than she wanted to admit. His jaw was rough with a day's worth of stubble. His lips looked incredibly soft, and when she looked into his eyes, she noticed just a hint of gold in those clear blue depths. Swallowing hard, she nodded.

But he didn't release her right away. And Penny certainly didn't feel any rush to move.

It was kind of the perfect moment, she thought. She had no idea what was going on outside, but inside, it was just the two of them and she felt like her heart was beating just a little too hard. Hopefully Spencer would think she was just nervous from almost falling and not from having her hands all over his inseam!

One minute passed, then two – at least that's what it felt like – when she finally took a step back. His grip didn't release easily and it was a thrill to think that he was as reluctant to let her go as she was to move away. "Um…thanks," she said softly, before walking over to the desk to mark down his measurements. "So…I think that's everything. I have all of your measurements noted and on file. Martin will have them here for you whenever Brett comes in with the rest of the groomsmen."

Her voice was slightly high-pitched and shaky

but…dammit, he made her nervous. Normally, Penny was extremely confident – especially at her job. And yet the last thirty minutes with Spencer had reduced her to a quivering mass of hormones!

Again.

There. She said it. She was nervous being around him and beyond turned on.

Busying herself at the desk, she figured he'd go get changed and leave. But he didn't. Instead he stood and simply watched her for a minute.

"Um…since you're not ordering tonight, you won't need to leave a deposit or anything. You'll just need to call and let Martin know when you're coming in again," she said, standing firmly behind the desk. Her grip on the desktop was enough to turn her fingertips white.

Nodding, Spencer walked toward her – slow and predatory – and her throat went dry. "I appreciate your help tonight," he said casually, and he looked so damn good in that tuxedo that she wanted to scream.

"Not a problem," she said as she attempted to straighten up the already-clean desk area.

"Are you ready to close up now?"

She nodded but focused on the stack of receipts that didn't really require any attention. "Yup. As soon as you're done, I can call it a day."

"Okay then," he said and then turned and walked back to the dressing room.

Penny almost sagged with relief when he was out of sight. This was ridiculous. She was embarrassed and mortified that she was reacting this strongly to him and kind of wished he would leave so she could breathe normally again. And maybe so her cheeks would stop feeling like they were on fire!

While Spencer was changing, Penny busied herself with putting things away and straightening up. Chances were she'd walk out with him – partly because it was late and she didn't like to walk out alone and partly because she was clearly a glutton for punishment.

Good to know your strengths and weaknesses.

He stepped out a few minutes later and handed her the tux he'd been wearing. Penny hung it on the rack behind her and shut down the computer. Without a word, Spencer stood and waited for her to finish and together they walked out of the shop. Gate closed and locked, she faced him.

"You don't need to hang around and wait with me. I'm going to stop back in at the bridal shop and check in with Hailey before I go. So...have a good night." There. That sounded good, didn't it? Not like she was trying to get rid of him or anything, she was just stating her intentions.

All Spencer did was nod as they both walked toward the exit. The bridal shop was the closest to the door and as they got closer, Penny's heart sank a little.

The gate was down.

The lights were off.

Hailey was gone for the day.

Dammit.

For a second, she was almost afraid to look at Spencer because she knew – she just knew – he'd be smirking. But when she looked at him, he had a very serene smile on his face.

"Have you had dinner yet?" he asked.

And her stomach decided to answer for her in a very loud, very unladylike growl. She let out a nervous chuckle and said, "Not yet. I was planning on picking up some takeout on my way home."

He nodded. "I was planning on doing the same."

Part of her got a little thrill in imagining that his definition of "same" was that he was planning on getting some takeout on his way to her place, but she knew that was just her overactive imagination at work.

Again.

They walked out the main doors and Penny set the alarm and locked up and she wasn't surprised when Spencer walked with her to her car.

Okay, this is crazy, she thought. Why is this so damn hard? It wasn't like Spencer was a stranger. They'd known each other for most of their lives. And did they have a history? Yes. Did that have to mean anything right now? Well…it did. It was the reason she was talking to herself so damn much lately. And if she really thought about it, there was nothing wrong with hanging out with a friend. She could totally think of him as just a friend.

If she tried really hard.

And on top of that, she thought – desperately trying to give herself an excuse for what she was about to do - he's not staying. He lives seven hours away. But…I really want to spend time with him.

Because this is how it always was – a little time with him was always better than none.

"I wasn't planning on anything spectacular," she blurted out. "Just some Chinese takeout if…if you'd like to join me."

The look of pure pleasure on his face at her invitation made her knees weak and as soon as his smile broadened to show his dimples, she knew she was lost.

And she didn't even have the will to care.

It wasn't until they were walking through Penny's front door that it really hit Spencer that he wasn't dreaming this.

She had invited him to join her for dinner.

At her home.

Alone.

Honestly, he had thought he was going to have to do a hell of a lot of convincing to even get her to agree to go out with him for dinner. Never did he even allow himself to imagine a scenario where she was the one to ask him out.

But he was certainly thankful for it.

Her condo was small but totally her. Everywhere he looked there were personal touches that made it feel like a home. His place back in Atlanta was nothing like this. Besides being about three times the size, it lacked…everything. Okay, that wasn't totally true – he had every upgrade and modern convenience, but his décor was more or less on the sterile side.

Funny how he never realized that before.

They worked together to set up the food and

Penny grabbed plates and utensils while Spencer poured them each a glass of wine from the bottle he'd picked up while they had waited for their food. Within minutes, they were ready to sit down and eat.

"Can you excuse me for just one minute?" Penny asked. "It's been a long day and as much as I love these shoes, my feet are killing me. I'm just going to get changed."

When she walked away, he felt a pang of regret. She looked incredibly sexy in her work attire – the form-fitting skirt, the sky-high heels…yeah, she had nearly knocked him on his ass tonight just by looking at her. And having her touch him while she was taking his measurements? He should get an award for not throwing her down on the platform and taking her right there so she could keep touching him.

Because she *had* touched him.

A lot.

Honestly, the first pair of pants and jacket had been fine. And so had the shoes. Spencer hid a grin as he thought about how he had simply said he wanted to try on another suit just to have an excuse to stay longer and for her to maybe touch him again.

And she had.

A lot.

Images of them from so long ago flashed in his mind – how they had progressed from innocent kisses and caresses to the wild and out-of-control frenzy the night of Eva's graduation party. Then he had to mentally shake his head because if he allowed himself to linger on those thoughts, he'd never survive dinner.

He was just about to take a sip of his wine when she walked back in.

She was barefoot and her toes were painted a very sexy shade of hot pink. As his eyes traveled up, he noted how she'd changed out of her standard attire of sexy skirt and heels and traded them for a pair of snug black yoga pants and a soft looking jade-green sweater. Her hair was loose and…

She was looking at him with an odd expression on her face.

"Spencer? Are you all right?"

He cleared his throat. "Um…yeah. Sure. Why?"

"I don't know. You just had a weird look on your face," she said as she sat down at the kitchen table. Spencer took the chair next to her. With a smile, she immediately reached for the container of shrimp lo mein. "Thanks for waiting, but I'm starving!"

She dug in with gusto and that was another thing he both remembered and appreciated about her – she loved food and wasn't shy about eating. Maybe it was because they had grown up together, but he'd never met another woman who enjoyed a meal quite like Penny.

The food was delicious and the conversation flowed. And even though they were sticking to safe topics – her job, weddings, his sister – Spencer knew he was enjoying every minute of it.

And from the smile on Penny's face, she was as well.

"So how come Brett sent you to look at tuxes?"

Placing his fork down, he looked at her and knew he had to come clean. "Okay, confession time," he began warily and noticed that her blue eyes went a little wide. "Brett didn't send me. Hell, he and Eva have no idea I even went to look at tuxes tonight. I did it on the off-chance that I'd get to see you."

Slowly, Penny put her own fork down and he watched her swallow hard. "But…how did you know I'd be in the men's shop tonight?"

"I didn't. It just sort of worked out that way," he said sheepishly.

"I don't understand…"

"I figured I'd use the tuxedo as an excuse to be at Enchanted and I planned on stopping in and saying hello to you and asking if you wanted to have dinner with me or even just coffee again."

Penny leaned back in her seat. "Wow."

"Maybe it wasn't the greatest plan but…I thought about you all week. And I get that you're hesitant with me and you have every reason to be but…dammit, I didn't want to leave things the way we…"

"Left them?" she finished for him.

"Exactly!" Then he paused. "Look, I don't think it's just a coincidence that we ran into each other again. And I don't know about you, but to me it still feels like there's something there. It's like we can slip right back into that place where we're laughing and having fun and…and after kissing you, I can't pretend that I don't want to try to see where things can go this time."

She gave him a patient smile. "Spencer, we've

been down this road enough times to know where it ends. I'd rather that we end this as friends this time."

"I've never kissed a friend the way I kissed you, Penny," he admitted gruffly and was pleased when she blushed.

"And I…well I don't kiss friends like that either but…" She paused and let out a loud sigh. "Okay, maybe we have some unfinished business and some left over…feelings. Maybe that's why this keeps happening."

That wasn't it and he knew it, but he wasn't going to argue with her at the moment.

"It's obvious that we're still attracted to each other," she went on. "So maybe there's just some lingering…sparks that we just need to get out of our systems so we can finally move on."

Spencer immediately straightened in his chair. "Um…I'm sorry. What?"

Nodding, she picked up her fork and took another bite of her dinner before she continued. "When are you heading back to Atlanta?"

If this was going where he thought it was going, he was going to say never.

"I'm supposed to head back…soon," he said vaguely.

She nodded again. "Okay. So what if we…spent some of that time before you left…together?" Penny was studying her plate and she was pushing her food around and he knew what she was saying – or trying to say – and seemed to be embarrassed about suggesting it.

Yeah. He knew her that well.

Rather than answer right away, he took another couple of bites of his own dinner. If he was reading the situation right, she wasn't simply suggesting that they hang out and talk. She was saying…everything he really wanted. And while he knew he should be jumping at this and not questioning it, the thought of leaving in…two days…was beyond unappealing.

Spencer knew he could take more time off – he could work from Raleigh just as easily as he could back in Atlanta. His hours were flexible and he wasn't punching a clock.

So why was he even questioning it or letting it play into the big picture?

Pushing his plate away slowly, he reached for his wine. After a sip, he softly said her name and waited for her to look at him.

He saw the vulnerability in her eyes and damn if he didn't want to do everything possible to ease it. "I think I would like that very much," he said and saw her visibly relax.

"Oh," she said breathlessly. "Oh…okay." And then she smiled at him and he knew she was feeling better about everything. "So…um…"

Standing, Spencer said, "Why don't we clear the dinner dishes and just…talk?"

Nodding, she came to her feet and started helping him.

They worked together washing dishes and wiping down surfaces as Spencer talked about his job – at Penny's request. He didn't mind talking about his work – it was something he was used to and comfortable with – but as they finished getting the kitchen back in order, he found that he didn't want to be talking about himself. He wanted to talk about them – about what was going to happen next.

Taking the dish towel from her hand, he placed it on the counter and then took her hand in his.

She looked at him curiously. "What?"

Slowly, he pulled her to him. "I promise we'll talk about whatever you want. I'll answer anything else you want. But I need to do this first."

And as was becoming their thing, he lowered his head and kissed her.

FOUR

She knew she should stop him, but…the man did amazing things with his lips and tongue and don't even get her started on how great his hands felt!

Penny knew she was in deep trouble and only sinking deeper. Spencer was becoming a bit of an addiction and that's why she boldly suggested having a fling with him just so they would have an excuse to keep doing this.

The kissing.

The touching.

She melted against him.

The only difference between this time and the last time was that they weren't in the rain and there wasn't a reason to stop. She was in complete control of her senses right now and they were all screaming at her to take this out of the kitchen and at least into the living room.

And there were definitely some parts of her that

were screaming for the bedroom.

"Spencer…" she said breathlessly against his lips and he instantly stilled.

His breathing was equally ragged as he rested his forehead against hers. "Sorry."

Penny licked her lips and gave him a shy smile. "Don't be. I…I was just thinking that maybe we could go…" *To my bedroom…* "into the living room and sit down."

He immediately took her hand in his again and led her to the sofa. Damn. She was hoping he would have read her mind instead.

As soon as they were sitting down, she could tell he was going to say something, but she wasn't ready to talk yet. She was still catching her breath from their kiss and she wanted to lose it all over again. Without a word, she reached up and cupped his cheek and brought his lips to hers again.

Oh yeah, she thought. *This is so much better than standing in the kitchen. Or the rain. But still not as good as my bed.*

They kissed until neither could breathe.

They stretched out until Penny was beneath him.

They touched everywhere their hands could reach.

And it wasn't enough.

Wrapping her legs around Spencer's hips, she arched up against him – silently pleading for more. More touching, more kissing, more…everything.

When his lips left hers, he kissed her cheek. He nipped at the shell of her ear and sighed her name.

"I think…" she panted, "I want…"

Lifting his head, Spencer studied her as he swallowed hard. "I can't believe I'm going to say this."

And she knew exactly what his next words were going to be…

"Then don't," she said breathlessly.

But he reared up and moved off of her until he was sitting at the far end of the sofa. "I really think we need to talk a little more and make sure we're on the same page and…" He turned his head and looked at her. "I don't want there to be any regrets."

Regrets? He could think about regrets right now?

Slowly, Penny moved to sit up and took a minute to get her breathing back to normal. "Okay, um…"

"Here's the thing," he quickly jumped in. "Right now, we're both a little on edge and immediate gratification would be awesome, believe me. But we're not strangers, Penny, and as much as we're sitting here saying that this is going to be a quick…you know…I don't want you to look back and hate that you made a rash decision."

"You think I'm making a rash decision?" she asked incredulously.

"What?! No! That's not…I mean…" Then he let out a long breath. "Okay, yes. I think we're both looking to make a rash decision."

And while Penny knew that statement should have been like a bucket of ice water being thrown at her, it wasn't. If anything, it made her want to be…reckless. Their time together was already going to be short, so why waste it talking about how they might feel afterwards? She already knew there were going to be regrets and there was no clear winning scenario here. If she jumped into bed with him, she was going to have regrets. If she didn't give in and sent him home right now instead, she was going to have regrets. Shouldn't they take advantage of what little time they had and use it to the fullest?

Sighing loudly, she said, "Wow."

Beside her, Spencer's shoulders sagged. "Yeah."

They sat in awkward silence for several minutes before Penny thought of something to say. "As you mentioned, we're not strangers. This isn't our first rodeo, Spencer," she said lightly, logically. "We're both adults who know what we want. I think we both may feel a little regret when it's time for you to leave and head back to Atlanta, but in the long run, we'll see that this was exactly what we needed to do and eventually be able to look back with no regrets."

Then she inched toward him ever-so-slightly.

"I don't know if I agree with that," he said gruffly, staring at his clasped hands.

She moved a little bit more.

"Spencer, we have tried this so many times that we can't argue the end result. And you know what? There's nothing wrong with admitting we're physically attracted to each other, just like there's nothing wrong with acting on that attraction."

He turned and looked at her and she wasn't sure if she saw gratitude or sadness in his eyes.

She opted for gratitude and moved even closer, noting how his eyes widened a bit.

"Do you want me?" she asked.

His immediate response was a small laugh. "You're joking, right?"

Now she was sitting practically hip to hip with him. "We keep starting and stopping," she said, her voice a little soft and breathy. "I'd like for us to start and...keep going." Leaning in close, Penny boldly nipped at his earlobe before adding. "Please, Spencer."

"Where's the bedroom?" he growled, low and deep and oh-so-sexily in her ear.

"Upstairs," she said and then gasped as he stood and quickly pulled her to her feet. "Spencer, I..."

She never got to finish because he scooped her up into his arms and kissed her again.

And then she forgot what she was going to say because he was on the move and she was a little in awe of literally being swept off her feet. When his lips left hers so he could focus on moving up the stairs, Penny's mouth went to work on licking and tasting any of his skin she could reach – his throat, his jaw – and simply savoring it.

She didn't realize they were even in her bedroom until Spencer lowered her to the bed. He didn't follow her down right away. Instead he was watching her intently. Penny was about to question it when he spoke.

"You realize what's different about this, don't you?" he asked softly.

She shook her head.

Putting one knee on the bed as he said, "This is the first time in all our history together that I'm going to get to make love to you all night."

Oh my…

And he was right. When they dated as teens, there had been no spending the night together and the last time they had "slept" together, it had been in the bathroom of his parents' pool house.

Hot as hell, yes. But she knew that this…what they were about to do…was going to be a million times better.

He peeled his shirt up and over his head before he leaned down and kissed her. This time it was slow, sweet and seductive.

Perfect.

Penny slowly wound her arms around his shoulders and guided him down to her. When Spencer was stretched out over her, his weight on her was like a delicious brand of foreplay all on its own. She felt like everything was right in her world, like she had been waiting forever for this – this one moment with him.

And somewhere in the back of her mind, she knew that was true.

And then immediately pushed that thought aside because it was too deep and too distracting for her to think about.

He lifted his head again. "Tell me I can stay the night," he whispered.

Her smile was just a little shy. "You can stay the night."

Kissing the tip of her nose, he said, "Tell me I can stay the weekend."

There was no hesitation. "You can stay the weekend."

Pulling back a bit, he stared into her eyes before he reached up and took off his glasses. As she watched him, she knew she'd give him whatever he asked for. If he asked to stay forever, she'd readily agree.

It was foolish – to fall again so hard and so fast – but there were things you couldn't change, couldn't fight. And this was one of them. From the time she was six years old she knew she belonged to Spencer Buchanan. And deep down, Penny knew that when the weekend was over and he went back to his life in Atlanta, there would be no recovering from the heartbreak.

And still she knew that she wouldn't change what was happening right now for anything.

He was worth it all – the love and the heartache.

❧

To say that life was perfect would be an understatement.

Saying it in reference to the last twenty-four hours would really be an understatement.

With a sigh, Penny snuggled closer to Spencer as their skin cooled and their breathing slowed down.

Yeah. It had been an amazing night.

And day.

And evening.

Penny's stomach growled and behind her,

Spencer chuckled. "I really wish more places around here delivered," he said as he nuzzled her neck.

"You and me both. We finished the last of the Chinese food earlier and other than some yogurt and tortilla chips, I don't have much to offer."

"That's where you're wrong," he said gruffly. "You have everything."

And damn if things like that didn't make her heart skip a beat.

He'd been saying them ever since they came up to the bedroom last night and with every word, every kiss, every touch, Penny fell back in love with him a little more. She didn't even think it were possible and yet...here they were.

It was just supposed to be about sex – a fling, a chance to get each other out of their systems. But she had seriously miscalculated just how strong her feelings were for him. And as Spencer continued to kiss and caress her, and as she tried chanting in her head that it was just sex, she knew she was nothing but a liar.

"How about we shower and go grab something to eat?" he suggested.

"You mean go out? Leave here?" she asked as she shook her head. "Nope. Can't do it. I want to stay right here."

He laughed again. "Believe me, I hate the thought of leaving here more than you know, but...I think we can both agree that we need food."

And right on cue, both of their stomachs growled.

Laughing, they rose from the bed and when

Spencer stretched, she couldn't help but stare. His body was lean and perfectly sculpted, and it distracted her just enough that all thoughts of food were quickly forgotten.

"Oh no you don't," Spencer said when she took a step toward him. "We are going to be responsible adults and go eat dinner."

She pouted. "Fine. But if I'm too tired to do anything else but come back and go to sleep, you have no one to blame but yourself."

And then she was in his arms and he was kissing her soundly. When he lifted his head, he smiled down at her. "And if I get to hold you all night while you sleep, it will still be worth it."

Dammit.

How did he do it? How did he always know exactly what to say to make her go all boneless?

"So…a shower, huh?" she asked.

He nodded. "You go first because if we go in there together we aren't leaving the house and we'll starve to death."

"There's always the yogurt…"

Laughing, he shook his head. "Can't stand the stuff."

"I think I might have some salsa to go with the tortilla chips. Maybe some guacamole…"

"Tempting, but I'm still taking you out," he said and gave her a playful shove toward the bathroom. "Go."

This time she didn't protest because she really was hungry and the thought of a shower was equally appealing. And when she went to close the bathroom door, she was happy to see that Spencer had watched her the entire time.

❧

They were eating at a small Italian place downtown an hour later and as much as he hated taking time away from having Penny alone and in his arms, Spencer knew this was good too.

Making love to her had been even better than he remembered and better than it had ever been with anyone else. Last night they had talked about their first time together which had – ironically – been the first time for them both. They had perfected things over time and yet he still felt that same wonder as he had the first time he made love to her. They were so in sync with each other and yet for all their years apart, it felt brand new and familiar at the same time.

"Okay, I'm sorry I fought coming out to eat because this is amazing," Penny said from beside him. She had ordered eggplant rollatini with spaghetti and the portion was huge; the smile on her face showed just how much she was enjoying it. "There may or may not be leftovers. I make no promises." Looking around the room, she said, "Maybe we should order an extra dish or two to go for tomorrow."

He laughed and took a bite of his fettuccine alfredo. He knew exactly what she meant because he was feeling a little doubtful that there'd be anything left of his food to take home.

"I was thinking we'd stop at the grocery store on the way home and get some things and maybe swing by my parents' place so I can get a change of clothes," he said. "What do you think?"

"The grocery store? Great. But stopping to see your folks...?"

"They would love to see you," he said. "You know they've always liked you."

She shook her head. "It's not that. It's just...I don't know...it feels weird that we're essentially going to walk in there and be like 'Oh, hey! Hi! Don't mind us. We're just here to grab some clean clothes for our dirty weekend!'" She stopped and shuddered. "I'm not comfortable doing that."

He studied her for a moment and knew there was maybe more to this than what she was saying.

"It's not like we're going to go in there and do it on the dining room table," he joked, hoping to lighten the mood. "They already know I wasn't home last night so..."

She gave him a mildly annoyed look. "Aren't we a little bit old to be talking about checking in with our parents?"

Okay, this was clearly a sore spot for her and it wasn't worth upsetting her to keep at it.

"How about I just throw my clothes in the laundry tonight? Of course, that means I won't have anything to wear so..."

That seemed to do the trick.

"I think that's brilliant because I have plans to sleep in tomorrow and be very lazy the rest of the day," she teased. "I might go to my Zumba class on Monday and I will have to go to work, but only for a couple of hours."

"Why only a couple?"

"We're closed on Mondays, but Hailey holds our weekly staff meetings then so we're all up to date on what's going on with our current brides and bridal parties. Plus we have all of the owners of the other shops in the complex come in and brainstorm about upcoming events and promotions. My class is at seven and then I need to be to Enchanted by ten, but I should be done by noon, maybe one." She paused and took a sip of her wine and looked over at him. "What about you? Do you know what day you're heading back home?"

He'd confessed about how he should've gone back by now and how he hadn't made any specific plans for his return.

"I know I need to be back by the end of the week, but...I'm going to try to get as much done as I can while I'm here so I'm not totally behind. I only have my laptop with me so I'm at a bit of a disadvantage and can't get everything done that I need to."

She reached across the table and took one of his hands in hers. "Spencer, I don't want you missing work because of me. I knew going into this that you weren't staying. You have a job and a life back in Atlanta, just like I have one here. So if you need to get back, it's okay."

And his heart kicked hard in his chest. "Are you...do you want me to leave?"

She sighed. "That's not what I'm saying. I just want you to know that I understand that you have responsibilities. Neither of us planned on this so..."

He squeezed her hand tightly when she tried to look away. "Penny...look at me..."

She did but there was a sadness in her eyes that wasn't there a minute ago.

"I know we didn't plan on this and I have no idea what *this* even is, but I know what I want it to be."

Okay, he hadn't meant to go there just yet, but now that it was out there…

"I know last night we said this was about getting each other out of our systems, but…that's not working," he said honestly. "All we've accomplished in the last twenty-four hours is proving that there is way more here to explore and that I want you more now than I ever have."

He heard her soft gasp and wasn't sure if it was a good one or a bad one.

Please let it be good, he thought.

"I feel the same way," she said quietly, "but…that's always been the case for me, Spencer. My feelings for you were never in doubt. It's always been your feelings toward me as a person that…"

"I know, I know," he interrupted, mainly because he hated how much of an asshole he'd been. "It was never really about you."

Penny pulled her hand from his and looked at him curiously. "What do you mean?"

Raking a hand through his hair, he leaned back in his chair. "You were always so…so beautiful and confident and as much as I admired those things in you, they…well…they intimidated the hell out of me. When we first started dating, you have no idea how many people made snide comments to me about why a girl like you would want to date a geek like me."

"Seriously?"

He nodded.

"But…why would that bother you? There was nothing wrong with you!" she argued. "You were this super smart guy who had everything going for him!"

"No, I didn't. Do you know how hard I had to study? How much my parents forced me to study? Getting good grades wasn't an option; it was mandatory. Granted, I'm thankful for it now, but at the time it was a lot of pressure on me. I got grounded every time I got a grade lower than a B."

"I never knew. They weren't like that with Eva…"

He shook his head. "They're very old-fashioned – they didn't think it was as important for her to have the good grades and the options that I did. And Eva was involved in so many other extracurricular activities that kept them focused – dance, piano…I swear there were so many damn recitals that it bordered on ridiculous. Either way, it was totally backwards and wrong but…there it is."

"So all the times you told me…or broke up with me…?"

"It was me. Not you."

At the shocked look on her face, he realized just what he'd admitted.

"Penny…I…"

"Do you have any idea how much your words messed with me? My self-esteem?" she hissed, leaning in close so no one would hear. "I questioned everything about myself because you

made me think there was something wrong with
me!" Leaning back in her seat, she glared at him.
"I cannot even believe this…that you could be so
cruel."

"I'm sorry!" he said quickly. "I didn't
know…I didn't think…"

"Really? A smart guy like you didn't *think* that
his words would have some kind of effect on
someone? Especially negative words?" Her voice
was getting louder and now people were starting to
stare, but he'd be damned if he would say anything
right now that would sound like a criticism.

"I was a kid, Penny," he said in quieter tones.
"I was stupid and I wasn't thinking of anything
except myself! Is that what you want to hear? Is
that going to change anything?" Then he paused.
"If I could, I would go back and change it all,
change everything – every damn time I let you go –
but I can't. I can only sit here and apologize to you
and hope that you'll forgive me."

Their waitress came by and asked if they
needed anything and Penny asked for a takeout box
and the check.

Spencer did *not* take that as a good sign.

So they boxed up their dinners.

They didn't order anything to go.

And he paid the check.

They drove back to her place in silence – not
stopping for groceries – and he had no idea what to
expect once they got there.

"I don't think you should come in," she said
when they were in her driveway.

For most of his life, Spencer didn't stand up for

himself. He'd basically admitted to that over dinner. But this time, he was.

"That's not acceptable to me," he said reasonably.

"Excuse me?" she asked slowly as her gaze turned to his.

"You heard me. I think we need to talk this out. This is important and we need to talk it out like adults rather than two kids who just walk away."

Wrong. Thing. To. Say.

If anything, he could see the rage building in her as she stared at him incredulously.

"That is *rich* coming from you," she snapped.

And he owned it. "I realize that and I'm trying to rectify it. It would be easy to just walk away and then you could keep your previous opinion of me and I could leave and continue to beat up on myself, but to what end? I'm tired of this! I'm tired of all the walking away and denying what I want!"

"You're the only one who keeps you from having what you want, Spencer!" she cried. "I never wanted to walk away! I never wanted you to walk away!"

He was poised to argue with her some more, but not here. Not in the car. Not when there was so much hinging on what came next. "Can we please go inside and talk about this? Please?"

And for a moment, he thought she was going to deny him – them – but she gave him a curt nod and climbed from the car.

One hurdle crossed.

Who knew how many more were to come?

❧❧

It was amazing how suddenly calm she felt once they were back inside her condo. At the restaurant? That was a completely different story. All of the years of self-doubt were for nothing. *Nothing!* That was simply him projecting onto her, and Penny wasn't sure if she could just let that go.

In the end, it had pushed her to work harder and to be a better person but...there wasn't anything wrong with her before! And then she thought about all of the time they had missed out on as a couple because of this and it made her sad.

"Penny, talk to me," he said softly from a few feet away. "Please."

Where did she even begin?

She didn't want to fight. Not really. And it wouldn't accomplish anything. Like he had said earlier, it wouldn't change the past or where they were right now. So what was she supposed to do? Say?

"You hurt me, Spencer," she finally said and felt the sting of tears in her eyes. She was in his arms before she could blink. They'd never done this. He'd never seen the devastation he caused or seen her cry. And maybe this was what had to happen.

Without a word, he picked her up and carried her to the sofa. When he sat down, he kept her cradled in his arms and simply let her cry. He didn't offer empty words or platitudes; he just let her feel what she was feeling.

She cried because of the words he had spoken

to her back then.

She cried for all of the time they had lost together because of misplaced feelings.

But most of all, she cried because she had no idea if they were really meant to be together right now.

Or ever.

When Penny finally lifted her head, she had no idea how much time had passed. She was emotionally wrung out and even though Spencer hadn't shed a tear, the look of devastation on his face told her he felt the same way.

"I'm so sorry," he said, his voice low and gruff. "I can never make that up to you. Ever. The things I said and did were…they were awful, and I hurt you. And I never wanted to hurt you. Ever. You don't deserve that."

She let out a long breath and contemplated her next words. "How do I know it's not going to happen again? How can I possibly trust that you're not going to feel pressured over something and take it out on me or our relationship?"

He went to answer but she quickly interrupted.

"That's why this needs to just stay as this – the weekend. I've come too far and I'm in a really good place in my life and I can't take that risk that you're going to undo all that I've done to build myself up. I just can't."

And then she saw them.

The tears.

And they were her undoing.

Leaning forward, she cupped his face in her hands and kissed him – pouring everything she had and everything she felt into it – and was relieved when he not only responded, but took over.

She needed this. It was wrong and the timing sucked but…if all she was getting was the weekend, then she wanted every second of it spent like this – wrapped up in each other, letting the past stay in the past and knowing that there was no future.

The present was going to have to be enough.

Every part of her was pressed against him and she did her best to keep it that way – arching, rubbing, wrapping. Her hands raked up into his hair right after she took his glasses off his face and flung them onto the coffee table. Spencer's arms were like a vice around her and his own hands seemed to be everywhere – on her back, anchored into her hair, grabbing her ass…

And it still wasn't enough.

Penny crawled off of his lap and maneuvered them until they were lying down with Spencer on top of her. She needed to feel him – all of him – to keep her grounded in the moment. There would never come a time when she wouldn't remember what he felt like stretched out over her – the feel of his muscles, the heat of his skin and how hard he was all over.

They kissed hungrily and desperately as clothes slipped away and they were coming together like they never had before. It verged on violent and even in their most frantic of moments in the past, it wasn't like this. It was never like this. This was the kind of act that was meant to make a memory – an impact.

She clawed at his back even as he bit and

growled and left his own marks on her pale skin. Madness and heat. Cries of love and pain. It all mixed together and seemed to go on forever.

But eventually heartbeats calmed and skin cooled.

And in the dim light of the living room, there wasn't anything either of them could say.

How were you supposed to say goodbye to the other half of your heart?

"Good morning! I'm Julianne and this is Zumba! Do we have any first-timers here today?" Julianne asked as she began her spiel. Several people raised their hands. "Awesome! I am so glad you decided to join us today! This is a cardio dance class but don't worry if you don't have any dance experience - you don't need any. And don't worry if you don't pick up the steps right away because we've all been there!"

It was seven o'clock on Monday morning and Penny was at the gym for Zumba. Not that she wanted to be, but it was the perfect escape and right now that was something she desperately needed.

Spencer had left an hour ago. There was no talk of staying in touch or anything regarding their future. They had simply said goodbye. Part of her expected more of him – like that he wasn't willing to accept that what they had was over. That was what he led her to believe while they were at dinner Saturday night. But after she had said her piece, it was as if he had given up.

And she wasn't sure if she was relieved or saddened by that.

After their romp on the sofa, they had gone to the bedroom where he simply held her all night long. There was no seduction; they'd silently agreed just to sleep. Sunday morning, Spencer had gotten up and gone out to get her groceries and pick up a change of clothes for himself before coming back. It seemed odd that he hadn't just left – that they hadn't just said goodbye right then and there – but clearly they were both gluttons for punishment because they spent all day Sunday watching movies and being lazy and then made love again all Sunday night.

All while acting like polite strangers.

It was maddening.

So right now, she needed this Zumba class and as the music picked up, she was more than happy to give it her all. And when it was over, she'd shower and get changed and go to her meeting at Enchanted. Then, even though it wasn't on the agenda, she was going to be bold and put forth her business plan for her glam squad.

And when all of that was through, she'd go home and kick, scream and cry because for a brief moment this weekend, she thought she could have it all.

FIVE

A week later, Spencer was miserable.

Still miserable.

Looking around his office, everything felt…wrong. He let out a weary sigh and leaned back in his leather chair. They'd been close…so damn close to making it work and he'd gone and screwed it up.

Well, technically you've been doing that for the better part of twenty years. Why stop now?

He hated when his conscience was right.

And now that he was back in Atlanta and back to his regularly scheduled life, he hated it. He hated every damn second of it. When he'd walked through the doors to his condo Monday night, it felt barren and sterile and completely unwelcoming.

And he remembered Penny's warm and welcoming home.

When he came into work on Tuesday, he spent the entire day holed up in his office because he didn't feel like socializing. No one asked how his trip was or how his family was, and he didn't see anyone smiling or laughing.

And he remembered Penny's stories of how close she was with her bosses and her co-workers.

When he got home on Wednesday, there was a wedding invitation from one of his oldest and dearest friends – along with an invitation to be a part of the bridal party – in the mail.

And there was Enchanted Bridal's business card tucked inside.

He wasn't sure if it was a sign he should go back for Penny or if the universe was mocking him.

His parents hadn't asked why he was leaving so suddenly, which was odd considering he had talked to them about Penny when he'd run in to grab a change of clothes on Sunday. If they noticed that he was upset or that anything was wrong, they didn't let on. And for that he should be thankful, but he wasn't. Right now he would welcome someone calling him and telling him how badly he had messed up the best thing that ever happened to him.

Again!

He needed it. He almost craved it in the most insane way!

And that's when he knew what he had to do…

Picking up his phone, he called his sister.

"Give me one good reason why I should talk to you," Eva demanded when she answered the phone and for a minute, he was confused. Then he figured his parents must have not only noticed something was wrong, but shared it with his sister.

"And good afternoon to you too," he said pleasantly. "How are you?"

"How am I? Seriously?" she cried. "I'm ticked off, Spencer! I had an appointment to try on gowns at Enchanted on Saturday and I saw Penny! And surprise, surprise, I had to say – yet again! – that I'm sorry that my brother is such a colossal jackass!"

Yup. This was what he needed, what he deserved.

"I know, I know and…"

"Shut up," she snapped. "You don't get to talk right now, because I'm talking." She let out a very long and agitated sigh. "How could you have screwed this up? Again!"

"It was…"

"I was *so* excited when I left you guys together the night of the fashion show! I saw the way you looked at her and the way she looked at you and…I just *knew* things would be different this time!"

"I did too and…"

"Then I get a call from Mom last Sunday and she was so excited because you were spending time with Penny, but she said that it seemed like you two had some things to work out. She was so optimistic. And so was I!"

"I was too…but…"

"So imagine my surprise when I got a call from her the next day saying you *left* and you looked upset – 'utterly devastated' were her words. I thought about calling you, but I was too angry. Then I thought about calling Penny, but I was too embarrassed. So I had to wait almost a week before

I saw her and instead of focusing on finding my dream wedding gown, I had to feel bad because one of my oldest friends looked so sad and I knew it was your fault! What the hell did you do?"

"Are you going to let me answer that question?" he asked but there was no power behind his words. He was too tired and defeated for that.

"Fine. Speak. But know that I reserve the right to interrupt and yell at you."

He couldn't help but chuckle at her honesty. "I would expect nothing less."

"Just so we're clear…"

And to her credit, Eva let him speak. Hell, she let him speak for almost ten minutes as he recounted most of what had happened between him and Penny from the night of the fashion show to the morning they said goodbye. Of course he'd left out the intimate details, but he knew she understood what he was talking about. When he was done, he let out a long weary breath. "And that's it. That's how I managed to screw it up again."

"Wow."

"I know."

"So…all those things you said to her back when you broke up…?"

"Not one-hundred-percent accurate."

"Damn, Spencer. Do you have any idea how self-conscious she got after that?" Eva asked. "I mean, I was probably the only one who noticed it but…damn."

"At the time, it didn't seem like a big deal…"

"For such a smart guy, you are incredibly stupid. You know that, right?"

"Eva…"

"You're the reason Penny stopped coming over. You're probably one of the main reasons she and I drifted apart." She snorted with disgust. "And you know what? You're my brother and I love you, but right now I really hate you."

"I know."

"Don't you have anything else to say for yourself?" she demanded.

Okay, this was not helping him feel any better. If anything, it was like rubbing salt in the wound. "I can only say I'm sorry so many times, Eva. The damage is done and there's nothing I can do to change that. I can promise till my dying breath that I'll never do it again, but she's always going to be wary and waiting for me to screw up again. That's not fair to either of us."

"I hate how that makes sense," Eva said, and Spencer had no doubt that she was pouting. "I want to yell at you some more and tell you what a moron you are, but…seems to me you are already well-aware of it. Kind of took the fun out it for me. Yelling at you now would just be mean."

"But well deserved."

"Obviously," she said followed by a sad sigh. "I wish I knew what to say here."

Spencer swallowed hard. "How was she? When you saw her on Saturday…was she all right?"

"No, Spencer. She wasn't all right," Eva replied calmly. "She looked sad and…and it was like she didn't want to even be near me or talk to me. It was awful."

He raked a hand through his hair. "Need I

remind you that you hadn't seen or talked to her in years? So you're kind of being a little dramatic."

"Look, I get it. I wasn't the greatest friend to her and I let the relationship go too because…well…I honestly don't know. People just drift apart. But after seeing her again and seeing the two of you together, I was really excited about reconnecting with her. That's not going to happen now."

"I don't see why not," he countered. "There's no reason why the two of you can't be friends again. You managed to stay friends in the past when I…"

"When you were a total jackass? Um…yeah, I know. This time was just…it was different, Spencer. Back then, we were young. We were kids. We were a little more resilient. But now? I don't know. It's harder when our hearts get broken. If anything were to happen between me and Brett, I know I'd be devastated."

"That's not a fair comparison. You and Brett are in love; you're engaged and getting married. Penny and I…"

"Oh, please. Everyone knows she's been in love with you since forever and if you pulled your head out of your ass once in a while, you'd realize that you're in love with her too."

Damn. That was…brutally honest and…totally true.

"It doesn't matter, Eva. There are too many obstacles here. I work and live in Atlanta. Penny works and lives in Raleigh. She's getting ready to open her own business. If we were going to do this and have a relationship, I sure as hell wouldn't want it to be long-distance."

"Penny's opening her own business? She didn't mention that to me."

"Probably because she didn't want to talk to you, remember?" he asked with just a hint of sarcasm.

"Very funny. So what's this business? Is it wedding-related?"

Spencer told his sister all about Penny's glam squad and just talking about it brought a smile to his face. He could picture her doing it and making it a place that people would flock to. She was that type of person – people were drawn to her and Penny had a gift for making everyone around her feel special. No doubt her customers would love her.

"That sounds like such a fun business! Oh my gosh! I'm totally going to hit her up to do the hair and makeup for my bridal party on the day of the wedding and mine too, of course."

And as much as he knew she meant well, Spencer had a feeling Penny wouldn't feel quite so excited at that particular prospect. But he chose to keep that to himself for now.

"You can't just give up, Spencer," Eva said, interrupting his thoughts. "You have to find a way to make this right!"

Seriously? After all the ways she'd just called him an idiot she thought he could even do that?

"How, Eva? Please tell me because I've been wracking my brain here for a week and I haven't got a damn clue. I thought it was best to just…stay away. Let her have her life and be happy without me messing it up."

"Oh, please, now who's being dramatic?"

"It's the truth."

"Well…I do kind of have an idea," his sister said slyly.

"But…?"

"But…if I tell you and you're open to it, you have to do exactly what I say."

He chuckled even as he shook his head. "Just regarding Penny, right?"

"Spoilsport."

"I'm not making any promises or anything, but I'm willing to listen."

She let out a little squeal of delight. "If you really want to win her back, this is where you need to begin…"

∽∾

"And that's what I can bring to the Enchanted Bridal complex," Penny said as she smiled at her bosses and Mrs. James – Hailey's mother and the woman who created Enchanted Bridal.

The five women sitting in front of her were all smiling.

Mrs. James stood first and came over and hugged her. "Penny, I think what you're offering is perfect for the complex. Of course, if you needed some time to get financing, we could always find a creative way to transform some of the existing space here in the shop for you to have a hair and makeup station."

Penny shook her head but kept her smile in

place. "Thank you, Mrs. James, but I don't think that would present the right image – not for the shop and not for what I have to offer. As of now, I can operate as a mobile business and go to the client's home, but that has its limits. In order to keep with the tradition of superior business service like what you've created here with the dress shop and then the complex, I wouldn't start doing promotions until I had the space secured."

"Have you heard from the bank?" Hailey asked as she stood and reached for a bottle of water.

"Not yet," she said with regret. "I know they said fast approval, but…this doesn't feel very fast at all."

Judith James placed a hand on Penny's arm. "It never does when you're the one waiting for an answer. I'm sure you'll hear from them any day now."

She hoped so, like seriously hoped so.

What she hadn't shared with her bosses was that her meeting with the bank had been met with less than an enthusiastic response. It didn't seem to matter that she had letters from Hailey and all of her bosses regarding their excitement to have Penny be part of the complex. It didn't seem to matter that she had a business proposal that met every criterion. What did matter was that she had some debt from her student loans and on her credit cards – more than they were comfortable with. And while they hadn't said that it would affect her loan application, she wasn't stupid.

Hailey, Becca, Angie and Ella had heard her proposal a week ago just like she'd planned. Her reason for doing it again today was strictly for Mrs. James' benefit. And while she was glad to do it, all she felt right now was more anxiety about not hearing back from the bank yet.

At least it was something other than the depression she'd been feeling over missing Spencer.

Not that it was going to go away any time soon.

He hadn't called. Or texted. He'd held true to his word that he was going to respect her wishes and stay away. And with every day that passed, she hated that about him.

It sucked being fickle.

But was she? Was that all it was? She didn't think so. Trust was a big thing to her and in the heat of the moment, Penny couldn't imagine trusting Spencer again.

Or trusting herself.

"Quick, give her something to do. She's getting that look again," Angie said in a mock whisper.

"Oh, leave her alone," Hailey replied. "She's allowed to have that look. Hell, we've all had that look so…"

"And when we did, our friends distracted us," Angie argued lightly. "Penny! Come with me. I've got something for you to do."

Penny snapped out of her wayward thoughts and saw Angie walking out of the shop. With a curious look to her remaining bosses, she saw they were just as confused as she was. With a shrug, she followed Angie out into the main hallway and then down toward the tuxedo shop. At the entrance, they stopped.

"I don't get it. What are we doing here?"

"Okay, here's the deal," Angie began. "Martin wants to take his wife out for their anniversary tonight, but Dan called in sick. He asked if one of us could help out and we of course said yes, but Ella's not feeling great and so we're going to close up early down there."

"Is Ella okay? I didn't know…I didn't notice…"

Angie waved her off. "She's just ready to have this baby. She really shouldn't even be here but she said she wanted a distraction."

"So why close the shop early? I'm sure you could call someone…"

"It's not a big deal. We don't have any clients booked for tonight and we're really just closing an hour earlier than usual. The girls and I are going to take Ella out to walk the mall – the big mall, not this one."

"Why?"

"Walking can induce labor and before you ask, we got her husband's permission to do it," she said with a laugh. "Anyway, we suggested that Martin just close early too but…he wasn't on board with that. If you'll stay, I'd feel better because should a random bride come in, you could sort of handle both places – you know, lock up the tuxes and open the dress shop or at least have your tablet with you to make an appointment. So? What do you think?"

The last time she'd volunteered to do this, she had spent the time with her hands all over Spencer.

"Oh, God…not the face again," Angie said with exasperation. "Seriously, enough with the face!"

From anyone else, Penny would be offended. But coming from Angie, she knew it was meant with love.

"I can't help it," she said miserably. "I just…I miss him."

"Dammit…I know you do," Angie said quietly and then reached out and hugged her. "And I hate that for you."

"I know it will get better but right now…?"

"It just sucks."

"Exactly."

They stepped apart and looked into the tuxedo shop. "Come on. Let's see what Martin has planned for you so we can send him on his merry little way to be one of the good guys."

Normally the thought of anyone being one of the good guys would put a smile on her face, but right now it just made her a little sad that she didn't have a good guy of her own.

Probably never would…

"The face," Angie sang quietly beside her.

Unfortunately, the only way to get over making the face was to focus on something else, and as she looked around the shop, she found it. Anger. The place was a bit of a mess and once again, Martin was bailing with no staff of his own to cover for him. She gave Angie a look that clearly spoke volumes.

"Yeah, I know, and we're working on it. Trust me." And then with a smile and a wave, she was gone.

Thirty minutes later, Penny was swamped. It

seemed that as soon as Martin left, madness set in. He'd explained about the two parties that were coming in for fittings and she couldn't help but be even more annoyed that he didn't have a better solution to his staffing problem than to dump it all on her.

She was going to have some strong words with Hailey and Angie about this tomorrow.

Six groomsmen in the first party – and they each had to be fitted and measured and have their information cards filled out. They were rowdy and more than a little distracted – not at all interested in the proper fit of a tuxedo. On top of that, she was mildly uncomfortable being the only woman in a room full of men. Luckily, she got through it and managed to keep a smile on her face the entire time. By the time they left, she felt like she ran a marathon.

One more hour…

Then the next group began to arrive.

With her smile in place, she immediately began to greet them and started to direct them to the rack Martin had set up for them when…Spencer walked in.

Her heart kicked hard at the sight of him and she wanted to scream for everyone to leave.

His name came out before she could stop it.

Smiling, Spencer said, "Penny Blake, this is my future brother-in-law, Brett Adams. Brett, this is Penny."

Shaking her hand, Brett smiled. "Eva's told me a lot about you. She didn't mention that you worked here in the tux shop, though."

"Oh, well…I'm just filling in for Martin," she said, trying to keep a pleasant smile on her face. Doing her best not to stare at Spencer, she immediately began to talk about the tuxedoes. It was a great distraction but not one that she wanted at the moment. "There's a rack outside the dressing rooms with tuxes for you to begin with."

The group of men all went in the direction she had pointed to and with a glance over her shoulder, she looked at Spencer as he walked with Brett back toward the dressing rooms.

❧

That was way harder than he thought it would be.

Seeing Penny had Spencer wanting to tell Brett and the rest of the groomsmen to get the hell out so he could be alone with her.

Patience.

Yeah, that's what his sister had told him. He had to have patience.

He'd waited almost another two weeks since his conversation with his sister before coming here, so that had to count as having patience, didn't it?

So he followed the rest of the guys to the back of the shop. And watched as Penny had her hands all over them.

While fighting the urge to kick everyone's ass.

It wasn't until everyone was in a dressing room trying on their suits that he finally approached her. "Hey."

Her smile was a little shy and her cheeks turned

the cutest shade of pink. "Hey."

"Do you still have my card on file or do we need to do my measurements again?"

She turned and went through the files and then she turned around again and began typing on the keyboard and searching the computer to find his information. "Um…"

"What's the matter?" he asked.

"It's…it's not here. All of your measurements and information…I know I entered them!" She looked up at him. "Remember? You were standing right here! And I wrote everything down!"

"It's not a big deal, Penny."

The look on her face said otherwise.

"Spencer, I know I put all of that information in the right place. There are four other men who I have to do this for before I can leave and if I screwed this up with your stuff the last time, how do I know I'm doing it right this time?" Then she gasped. "What if the last group of guys who were in here a little while ago never get their tuxedoes? What if – because of me – that wedding gets ruined?"

Okay, she was starting to freak out and he walked around the counter and gently grasped her by the shoulders. "First of all, deep breaths," he said soothingly. "Second, did you write everything down?"

She nodded.

"Okay. You can either make copies of them all and set them in a separate folder or you can take pictures of the info on your phone or…"

Penny stepped back and let out a breath.

"You're right. You're right. This isn't a big deal." But before she could say more, the guys started coming out and she sprang into action, making adjustments and writing notes on their cards.

Spencer stood back and stayed behind the desk and let her work. She was quick and efficient and in no time, everyone was done.

Well…except for him.

As each of the guys paid for their deposit, he watched as she checked and double-checked and even triple-checked where she put everyone's information. She typed it into the computer, she wrote it down, and she copied it on the printer. When she was done, Penny seemed to sag with relief. Spencer waved to Brett, who gave him a thumb's up, and when the group was gone, he turned back to her.

"You okay?" he asked.

"I think so," she said with a weak smile. "I can't believe Martin doesn't have more help in here. That was a lot for one person to do – especially someone who doesn't work here on a usual basis – but thank God I'm done."

"Not quite," he said and gave her a lopsided smile.

Rather than answer him, she said, "Those measurements have got to be around here somewhere. I know it." Then she began searching all of the files again and scanning and scrolling on the computer.

Not the best stroke to his ego.

For five minutes he watched her search every surface, every folder, and go back and curse at the computer when she didn't find what she was looking for. When she hung her head and sighed, he knew she was ready to admit defeat.

"Do you remember any of the measurements?" she asked wearily.

He did. And he gave them to her.

Penny went and grabbed two tuxedoes for him to try on and set them up in the dressing room. "See how those fit," she said quietly.

Nodding, he did.

The first one fit fine. And so did the second. But he stepped out and up onto the platform anyway. "I think we should confirm the measurements just in case," he said when she looked at him.

What followed was torture, pure and simple.

Even though she acted no differently than she had with the rest of Brett's party, Spencer knew her touch so well, was so attuned to it that it had all of his senses on high alert. Even the most innocent of touches practically had him reeling.

She didn't speak other than to ask him to move an arm or leg for her to get an accurate measurement but in his mind, she was asking for other reasons.

Dirty reasons.

Sexy reasons.

And now he was hard.

"That's everything," Penny said as she stepped away and quickly moved over to the desk. "We'll just need the deposit from you and then you'll be all set."

"Penny, I…"

"It's been a really long day, Spencer, and I'd like to go home. Please."

Okay, so that one sentence pretty much cut him down in every possible way. With a curt nod, he went and changed. When he was done, he paid the deposit and then silently waited for her to finish closing so he could walk her out. Neither spoke of it, but they knew it was what he was doing.

It wasn't until they were outside and Penny was locking up the building for the night when he cursed.

"What's wrong?" she asked.

Spencer was patting down his pockets and his jacket and then cursed again. "My keys," he said. "I can't find them."

She looked at him suspiciously. "Seriously, Spencer? This isn't funny."

Honestly, he wished he had been creative enough to think of something like this. But he hadn't. This was truly an innocent mistake. "Seriously," he replied. "They must have fallen out while I was changing."

Penny still didn't look like she believed him, but rather than argue, she unlocked the door and turned off the alarm. As soon as he stepped in, she locked the door behind them and then led the way back to the tux shop. She didn't turn on any of the main lights when they got there. Instead, she walked at a clipped pace – her stilettos making a very distinct clicking sound as she walked – toward the back and flipped on one small overhead light.

Spencer was right beside her and opened the dressing room door.

The keys weren't there.

What the hell?

"They're not here," she said, confusion lacing her voice.

"I know."

"But...where else could they be?"

He shrugged. "I have no idea. They were firmly in my pocket when I got here earlier..."

She glared at him with a huff of agitation. "Come on, Spencer. I don't have time for this. It's been a long day, I haven't had dinner and I really just want to go home, okay?"

"If I knew where the keys were, don't you think I'd have them?"

"Honestly? No. No, I don't. I think you're playing with me and trying to find a way to force me to spend time with you. Well let me tell you something. I don't think it's funny. It's mean. And if you care about me at all, just admit that you have the keys or pick them up wherever you hid them so we can go!" she cried.

And that's when he heard the tremor in her voice and saw her eyes growing shiny with tears.

Dammit.

He stepped forward and gently put his hands on her shoulders. "Look, I *do* want to spend time with you. I never said otherwise, but you have to know that I really have no idea where my keys are. I swear." He kept his tone soft and soothing and it broke his heart that she was looking so defeated. "I...I'll just call Brett and ask him to come pick me up."

"And then what?" she said quietly. "You still

won't have your keys."

Oh. Right.

"Come on," she said as she stepped away from him. "Let's look around. They have to be here somewhere."

Penny checked the pockets of the suits he'd tried on while Spencer scanned the floor around the dressing room. This was not how he planned it. Eva had told him to stay and walk her out, invite her to get some coffee – someplace neutral – and tell her how much he missed her. *Show her how much she means to you,* Eva had urged. All he'd managed to do was tick her off and make her work later than she wanted to.

Strike one on the Win Penny Back campaign.

When he turned and looked at her, she was looking under racks and he heard her curse. Then she came back by the fitting rooms and glared at him.

"Any luck?" she asked.

He shook his head. "I've looked all around here and then the path I walked from here to the platform and I can't find them."

"Dammit, Spencer!" she cried. "This is ridiculous!"

It was one of the few times she had really yelled at him. She was flushed and ticked off and a little breathless and…she was sexy as hell.

And for some reason, that just made him want to add fuel to the fire.

"You think I'm enjoying this? You think I want to stay here surrounded by tuxedoes while you get madder and madder at me?" he yelled.

"Because let me tell you, I can think of at least a thousand other things I'd rather be doing right now, and most of them are with you! And none of them involve arguing over a set of freaking missing keys!"

Her soft gasp was the only sound she made before turning and going to the dressing room he'd used. "They've got to be in here," she muttered.

Following her, he stepped into the small space and as soon as she saw his reflection in the mirror, she spun around.

Her breath was slightly ragged.

Her blue eyes went wide.

And those lush lips parted.

Spencer moved closer as Penny took a step back. Her back immediately hit the mirror and a small grin tugged at his lips.

"They're not in here," she said, her voice so soft it was a mere whisper.

"I know."

But the two of them were, and because she was already pissed off at him, he figured he better go big or go home. Before he had time to second-guess himself, he reached up, cupped her face and kissed her.

Penny offered no resistance. Her hands came up and gripped the front of his shirt to pull him closer. This was what he had fantasized about the first time he'd come here – of getting her alone in the fitting room and claiming her, making her his – and this time, he was doing just that.

SIX

Thank God.

That was the only thing Penny could think of as Spencer swooped in and kissed her.

For the last ten minutes it had been all she could do to keep her hands to herself, especially after going through the whole process of taking his measurements again. Normally she was able to detach herself from the task but with him, it was impossible.

Spencer's hands moved from her face down to her shoulders, her breasts – where they lingered just a bit – before reaching around and cupping her ass.

God does that feel good...

She rubbed against him and cursed the fact that her skirt was so snug and that they were both fully dressed.

Then his hands were on the move again, this time reaching down and slowly bunching her skirt up, up over her thighs and higher.

Yes...

When it was around her waist, his hand squeezed her ass as he lifted her. Penny readily wrapped her legs around him and cried out at the intimate contact.

Lifting his head, Spencer looked at her. "I wanted to do this the last time I was here," he said breathlessly.

"Me too," she admitted just before she leaned in and kissed him again. Over and over until they were desperate for air and still she wanted more. Breathing was overrated, right? Each time they came back for more, she didn't think it could be hotter or wetter than the last, but it was.

Suddenly, one of Spencer's hands wasn't on her ass, it was stroking her leg, smoothing over her skin. Her mind was screaming out all of the places she wanted his hand, his mouth, but she didn't voice them because it would mean breaking their kiss. So she waited and squirmed and moved in his arms hoping to guide him to where she wanted his touch.

And she fully believed he was a mind reader because his hand immediately moved – teasing at the silk of her panties. That's when she tore her mouth from his. "Yes," she panted. "Right there. Please."

"Look at me," he growled and in her half-dazed state, she did. "Tell me you want this."

"I thought I just did," she moaned, moving against him.

"Tell me it's okay that we're doing this here..."

Her head fell back as she ground it against the mirror. "It's totally okay..." she said breathlessly.

"Tell me…"

"Spencer!" she snapped as she straightened her head. "I swear if you don't do something right now I'll scream."

His smile was naughty and triumphant. "Sweetheart, you were going to scream no matter what. Trust me."

And within seconds, she did.

∾⋙∽

"Okay…just admit it. You didn't lose your keys."

Spencer chuckled softly as he finished straightening his clothes. "Unfortunately, I really did."

Looking over at her, he smiled at how beautifully mussed she was. Her hair was a riot of curls and her clothes were wrinkled and she'd never looked better to him.

"How is that possible? This store isn't that big."

"I have no idea. All I know is that I drove myself here and had my keys with me and now I don't." Then he stood and held his arms out at his sides. "Want to frisk me and make sure I'm not lying?"

"No," she said with a small laugh. "But you can't blame me for being suspicious."

And…he couldn't. But then he realized he had his own reason to be suspicious.

"What about you?" he asked as she was about to step out of the room.

Her eyes went wide as she looked at him. "What about me?"

He moved closer to her. "I think you knew exactly where my measurements were and you just pretended that you didn't so you'd have an excuse to…you know…measure me again." He waggled his eyebrows playfully as he teased her. Luckily, she didn't get offended.

Much.

"You know what? I wish that were the case," she admitted. "But I really couldn't find them anywhere and now I'm freaking out that I've screwed up tonight's orders." Then she shrugged. "Although, I did make the copies, I'm going to ask Martin to show me the whole procedure again just in case I have to sub in here again."

"Maybe he should just hire more help."

Nodding, Penny said, "Oh, I agree. Tonight was totally unprofessional of him. I get that he wanted to take his wife out – it was their anniversary – but being that he knew how many people were coming in, he should have stayed. As the owner, he should have stayed."

Spencer wrapped his arms around her waist and kissed her on the temple. "Personally, I'm glad he left."

She didn't answer, but she did let out a soft sigh as she relaxed against him and it felt pretty damn great.

It gave him hope.

Unfortunately, they still had to find his keys so they could leave and hopefully go somewhere to talk.

"Come on," he said softly. "We have keys to find."

Penny let out a little sound of protest before stepping away from him and then gave him a weak smile. "I know."

They stepped out of the dressing room and Spencer decided to take another look around the area while Penny walked over to the desk. "Maybe I should turn on the rest of the lights," she said and almost tripped.

"You okay?" he asked, immediately at her side.

She nodded and looked down and…there were the keys. When she went to retrieve them, Spencer stopped her and stooped down to do it himself. When he straightened, he dangled them and she let out a nervous laugh. "How did I miss them? I was looking right over here."

"And I looked over here earlier," he said.

Personally, he didn't care how or why she missed them; he was happy that she had. If they had found them right away, he had no doubt that she would be home and he'd be at his parents and neither would be feeling quite this good.

Leaning in, he kissed her softly on the cheek. "Come on. Let's get out of here. It's late and you're probably hungry."

She glanced at him and blushed slightly. "A little."

They walked in silence out of the building and – once again – she set the alarm and locked up.

"Spencer, I…"

He placed a finger over her lips to quiet her. "Let's go grab a burger or something at the diner and talk."

She stepped back and looked at him oddly. "Really? You...you want to go to the diner?"

Hell no he didn't want to go to the diner. He wanted to grab some takeout, go back to her place and stay there. But...they'd already done way more than they should have before sitting down and talking like they needed to. So he'd tamp down the need he had for her and be a gentleman.

For now.

His sheepish grin gave him away. "No. But...I think we should."

She laughed softly. "Normally I'd agree with you, but I'm a bit of a mess and I'm not really sure I want to go out anywhere. Would it be all right if we just grabbed something and took it back to my place?"

Well...if she was suggesting it...

"How about you head home and I'll pick something up and meet you there? This way you can get changed and relax for a bit. How does that sound?"

Her smile was instantaneous and full of gratitude. "Perfect. Thank you."

"Okay," he said with a nod. "You want fast food? Tacos? Chinese? Pizza?"

"Ooh...pizza! I haven't had that in ages."

"Pepperoni?"

"Like there's any other kind," she replied, still smiling.

"Done." And even though he wanted to lean in and kiss her, he didn't. "I'll go pick it up and be at your place in about an hour. Is that okay?"

"Definitely."

He waited until she was in her car and driving away before he left. It wasn't until he was driving that he realized he had no idea what to say to her when he got to her place. Everything he'd planned to say – like how they could take it slowly and really get to know each other again – flew out the window the minute he followed her into that dressing room

Not that he was regretting that move.

Not at all.

But now things were complicated. Again.

The entire drive to the pizzeria, he thought about it. The entire time he sat and waited for their pizza, he thought about it. And the entire drive to Penny's, he thought about it. And as he knocked on her front door, he realized that he still had nothing.

⚬⚬

Her phone was ringing as she walked in the front door. Fishing it from her purse, Penny looked at it and frowned, not recognizing the number.

"Hello?"

"Penny? Hey, it's Eva! How are you?"

It had been two weeks since she and Eva talked, but they'd texted a few times in an attempt to try to get together for lunch. "Hey! I'm good. And you?"

"Oh, you know, busy as ever." She paused. "Is this a good time?"

"Actually…I just walked in the door and…" Damn. Did she admit what her plans were for the night? Did she want to open that can of worms right now when all she wanted to do was get changed, relax and wait for Spencer?

"Penny?"

Oh, right. "I'm waiting for your brother to meet me here with a pizza."

Eva's squeal of delight made her pull the phone from her ear. "Thank God!" she finally cried. "I was hoping he wasn't going to chicken out!"

"Uh…chicken out?"

"Yeah," Eva said, sounding relieved. "I knew he went with Brett and the guys tonight for their tuxes and I was hoping he was going to come and see you."

"Well…he did," she said lightly.

"And now you're going to have dinner together! Yay!"

At least one of them was feeling that way. Right now, Penny's nerves were still a little all over the place and she was hoping to get her head together while she had some time to herself.

"So…wait. If you knew Spencer was coming to see me, why are you calling?"

Eva laughed softly. "I'm nosy. I admit it. Plus, I tried asking Brett about how it went and he was of no help. I figured I'd give you a quick call and see if you'd be willing to tell me anything."

Unable to help herself, she laughed too. "Then rest assured – Spencer did come to see me and we're going to sit down and talk over pizza."

"Okay, I know you just got home and I'm sure you want to get changed and all that…"

"But…?"

"But," Eva continued, her tone going a little somber. "I just want you to know that my brother…well…he's one of the greatest guys I know."

"Eva…"

"No, please. Let me finish." She paused. "He told me about the things he said and did back when you guys dated and you have to know how awful he feels about it."

It was nice that his sister was defending him, but Penny knew it really didn't concern Eva. She was about to say just that when her friend started talking again.

"I know he's apologized, but knowing Spencer, it wasn't the greatest apology."

"That's not it, Eva…"

"I know, I know. He went back to Atlanta because that's what you guys agreed on, but he's not happy. I know he's not."

Before Eva could go on, Penny stopped her. "I appreciate what you're trying to do here. I do. But this isn't an easy situation and it's something Spencer and I need to work through."

A heavy sigh was her only response.

"The fact that he's here and we're even trying to work things out is good, right?"

"I suppose."

Penny glanced at her kitchen clock and calculated that maybe she had another twenty minutes tops before Spencer arrived. There were things she needed to do before he got there. If it were any other time, she'd probably curl up on the sofa and talk to Eva for hours about what she was going to do, just like they did when they were younger.

But there wasn't time.

"I really need to go, Eva," Penny forced herself to say.

"Okay, I get it. But…just promise me something."

"Anything."

"Promise that you'll give him a chance."

Her mind raced and she knew without a doubt that she would do exactly as Eva asked.

And not just because she'd asked.

"I will. I promise."

With another promise to call her tomorrow, Penny hung up and immediately sprang into action. Kicking off her shoes and unbuttoning her blouse on her way to her bedroom, she cursed the precious minutes she'd lost while on the phone. Racing around, she quickly changed and did her best to try to figure out what she was going to say when Spencer showed up.

For the better part of an hour, she had been asking herself what the hell she was doing. She still couldn't believe she had just had sex with him in the tuxedo shop! What if Martin had cameras? What if everyone at Enchanted found out what she'd done?

Her heart was racing like mad when she heard Spencer's knock at the door. "A problem for tomorrow," she muttered as she padded to the door and let him in. She'd changed out of her work clothes and was now in a pair of flannel pajama pants and t-shirt. It was a comfortable choice, but she also hoped that it would act as some kind of armor to protect her from jumping him again.

The look on his face when she opened the door told her that her choice of clothing wasn't going to be a deterrent.

The pizza smelled delicious, but Spencer looked even better. His hair was a bit of a mess and the boyish grin on his face had her melting. "Come on in," she said.

They opted to set up and eat in the living room and neither spoke through their first slices. She had set up paper plates and drinks before he arrived and as she took a long drink of her soda, she knew she'd procrastinated long enough.

"Thank you for dinner," she said.

He smiled. "My pleasure."

Ugh...did he have to say pleasure? Like her mind wasn't already wandering in that direction?

"So..."

"So..." he repeated.

"Tonight was a little...intense," she finally said.

And he nodded in agreement.

"I wasn't expecting to see you again. I mean, I figured I might see you because of Eva's wedding and you coming in for your tux and all but..."

"I know. I know what you mean," he said slowly as he reached for one of her hands. "I didn't come there tonight for...well...for what we did. Although that was amazing."

Penny couldn't help but blush.

"But I also didn't want you to know I was coming and give you an excuse to avoid me."

"I wouldn't have…"

"Yes. Yes, you would have," he corrected lightly. "And I can't blame you."

She sighed quietly as her gaze met his. "What are we doing, Spencer?"

"I've been miserable," he said gruffly. "More miserable than I ever imagined. Everywhere I looked, I saw something that reminded me of you." He paused. "I missed you."

"I missed you too," she admitted. "But…there are still so many things…"

"I know," he said quickly. "I know there are and that's why I'm here – so we can talk about them and figure them out." When she started to speak again, Spencer held up a hand to stop her. "I think we deserve a chance to figure things out, Penny. Finally."

And the thing was, she knew he was right. She had been miserable since he left, too. She regretted her rash decision and her refusal to even consider moving forward together. After so many damn years of what ifs and maybes, didn't she deserve to find out where this could go? Hell, she'd been waiting for what felt like forever to try for her happily ever after with this man. Was she really going to give up now without a fight?

"I agree," she said, gently squeezing his hand. The look of relief on his face gave her a little hope. He wasn't just saying the words she wanted to hear; he really meant them. "But…"

Spencer placed a finger over her lips. "No. No 'but.' Not yet," he said. "For right now, can we please just enjoy the rest of our dinner and…I don't know…just talk about something neutral? Tell me about work. How has work been?"

Easy enough, she thought. She told him about some of their more difficult clients and about some of the new gowns that had come in before telling him about her afternoon with his family.

"Was my sister a difficult bride?" he asked with a chuckle.

Penny laughed with him. "Not at all. She found a gown that she loves and it needs minimal alterations so she was thrilled."

"And my mother? How much of a nightmare was she? I know she and Eva are butting heads over how fast this whole thing is happening," he explained. "We all know that Brett is being deployed and that's why everything is so rushed, but for some reason my mother can't seem to stop complaining about it."

"She did make a few comments, but Eva did a great job of distracting her. Hailey, my boss, caught on immediately and started pulling out some mother-of-the-bride gowns to help. All in all, it was a very good afternoon. Everyone was happy."

His gaze narrowed. "Really? Because that's not quite the version I got."

"What do you mean?" Looking back, Penny distinctly remembered both Eva and Mrs. Buchanan being happy with their dresses and leaving with smiles on their faces. "Is Eva not happy with her gown? Does she need to come back and find something else?"

He shook his head. "No, my sister is fine with all of her wedding stuff. She mentioned that you were upset, so that upset her and…let's just say I got a very angry lecture from her about our relationship."

Oh God, was that why he was here? Because he got pressured by his family?

Before she could comment on that, he was speaking again.

"Don't get me wrong, Eva didn't say anything to me that I wasn't already thinking, but…I hated that you were upset."

"Spencer, you knew I was upset. That shouldn't have come as a surprise to you."

He sighed. "I know but…I did what you asked. I guess I thought if I respected your wishes you'd be okay…happy…"

"I did too," she admitted quietly. "I just don't know how to make this work."

And she really didn't. Even if she was able to move on from her insecurities, it still left one very obvious issue with them moving forward – logistics.

"I'm not a fan of long-distance relationships either," he said, reading her mind. "But I think we can give it a try – at least for a month or two – and then talk about it some more. I'll come up on the weekends or we can switch it up and you can come down to Atlanta…"

"I only have one weekend a month off," she said. "And then there are the fashion shows on Friday nights. Plus, when I hear back from the bank, I'm going to be working on the new shop and…"

"You did it?" he asked excitedly. "You submitted your business plan? I didn't think you were going to do it so soon. What did everyone think?"

Penny immediately relaxed and for the next few minutes, she told him all about her presentations – both of them – to Hailey and the girls at Enchanted.

"And what about the bank? Were they impressed? You must have just talked with them because they make their decisions fairly quickly. I'm sure they're going to approve you."

"Well…"

"Uh-oh," he said, his expression sympathetic. "What happened?"

She explained about her student loans, credit cards and how the loan officer's immediate response to her business idea was less than enthused. "I'm trying to be optimistic," she said. "But…I'm kind of afraid that they're going to turn me down."

He pulled her into his arms and kissed her on the forehead. "I'm sure you have nothing to worry about."

As much as she wanted to mention how long she'd been waiting for a reply, she opted not to. It would only depress her and now that he was here, she didn't want to feel that way. They had more important things to talk about.

"How long are you here for?"

"With you? Um…"

She chuckled softly and snuggled closer to him. "I meant in town," she clarified. "It's Thursday so I'm guessing you're here through the weekend?"

Nodding, he kissed her again. "That was the

plan. But I can see about working remotely next week. I came a little more prepared this time, so I can get some things done and not fall behind."

"Are you staying at your parents' house?"

He nodded.

"You know you don't have to…"

Kissing her hand, he smiled. "As much as I love the way you think, it would probably be best if we slowed down a bit and spent some time doing normal things like actually dating."

"A little late for that, wouldn't you say?" she teased.

Spencer couldn't help but laugh. "It does seem a bit backwards but…I want to try and do this right. It would be so easy to just bring in my suitcase and stay here with you, but being in this little cocoon we've built for ourselves maybe isn't the healthiest thing for our relationship. We need to see what it's like to be a couple out in the real world."

His words made complete sense and she wasn't sure if she should be happy or disappointed. Just thinking of Spencer staying with her and having him all to herself was definitely appealing, but he was right. If they were going to put in the effort for this relationship, they needed to stop moving so fast.

"So…where does that leave us?"

For a moment he studied her. "I think we can sit here and relax tonight, maybe watch a movie and then I go back to my folks' house for the night. Tomorrow we can go out to dinner, maybe see a movie or see what Eva and Brett are doing and try a double-date."

"Ooh…now that does sound like fun. We've never done that before," she said, feeling excited and optimistic about all the possibilities.

"Then it's about time we tried that, right?"

His words, his smile…it all worked because for the first time since seeing him again, Penny had hope.

❧

They'd spent the weekend together doing some pretty mundane things like grocery shopping, binge-watching *The Crown* on Netflix and then going out to dinner with Eva and Brett on Saturday night. It was way more fun than she imagined and it didn't take long for her to start making plans with Eva for just the two of them. She'd missed her friend and didn't even realize it until they started catching up on each other's lives.

On Sunday, Spencer picked Penny up and took her to brunch before they went and walked around a local outdoor flea market. It wasn't something she normally did, but it was fun to just walk around and comment on what they thought people would do with some of the junk they saw there. Afterwards, they went back to Penny's and decided to make dinner together.

After they ate, she was loading the dishwasher while Spencer took out the trash. No doubt they'd watch some TV and then he'd leave. It was what they agreed upon but…did that mean that he was not allowed to spend the night with her? Ever? Wasn't it okay to maybe pick one or two nights a week that they were allowed to indulge? She sighed loudly and almost jumped out of her skin when she heard Spencer behind her.

"You okay?"

Turning, hand over her rapidly-beating heart, she faced him. "What?"

"I heard you sighing and thought something was wrong."

"Oh, um…it's nothing. I'm good." When she went to turn back to the sink, Spencer stopped her. Looking at him with just a hint of annoyance, she said, "I just want to get the last of the dishes in here. Why don't you go get the next episode of *The Crown* pulled up?"

"Uh-uh," he said, staring at her with just a bit of defiance. "Something's on your mind. I can tell."

Rolling her eyes, she said, "Okay, fine. Something's on my mind. There. Happy?"

He chuckled. "Only if you tell me what it is."

Ugh. How did she even explain it?

"Penny?"

"Okay, here's the thing – I was just thinking about how we were going to watch some TV and then you were going to go home."

"And…that made you sigh?"

She nodded.

"But…why?"

Choosing to ignore him for a minute, Penny finished loading the dishwasher and then slammed it shut before facing him again. "Because I know that we said we were going to slow things down, but I didn't think that meant we had to…you know…completely stop everything."

She could tell it took him a few minutes to catch on to what she was saying and then he started to grin.

And she wanted to slug him.

"Happy now?"

"As a matter of fact, I am," he said, crossing his arms over his chest. He continued to grin.

"Look, I've really enjoyed these last several days, Spencer, but I miss some of the other aspects of our relationship too. What if we just…?"

He held up a hand to stop her. "What if I told you I had an overnight bag in my car?"

A small smile played at her lips because she kind of had a feeling she knew what he was saying. "You do? But…why didn't you just bring it in when we got back earlier?"

He nodded again. "I didn't want to be presumptuous."

Penny pulled back and looked up at him. "Were you hoping to stay here tonight?"

Another nod. "I've enjoyed these last several days too, but…" He stepped in close and wrapped his arms around her waist. "You're very tempting, Penny Blake. And I want us to keep going in this direction, but I miss those other aspects too."

"It seems that neither of us have any self-control," she said even as she blushed at the admission. "It almost seems silly to pretend that we don't want to spend the night together."

Spencer seemed to sag with relief and then his expression turned bashful.

"What? What's the matter?"

His gaze met hers. "I kind of feel silly now. We should be able to talk about these things without it being so awkward, right? I mean, I should have just told you that I wanted to spend the night and dropped my bag off when I picked you up this morning." Then he paused. "Or…I should just leave some stuff here just in case."

"That would certainly be convenient," she said slowly. "But that may make things too convenient and we'll slip right back into our old patterns and never leave the house." Before he could say anything else, she kissed him soundly.

"I swear I wasn't trying to pressure you," he argued lightly.

"In case you've forgotten, I was the one who brought it up first so there's no pressure at all. Unless…unless I'm the one pressuring you."

"Never," he replied, caressing her cheek.

She hugged him. "Good. I'm glad you have your stuff here with you and that you won't be leaving tonight."

It was amazing how good it felt to say that.

Together they walked into the living room and sat down on the sofa. "But…"

"But…" he repeated.

"I do have to work tomorrow."

"You just have to go in for the weekly meeting, right?" he asked.

"Exactly. Plus I have Zumba."

"Zumba?"

She nodded. "It's a cardio class I take at the gym. I started taking it about six months ago and I love it. It's all different kinds of dancing and it's an insane workout, but I try to go to at least three classes a week."

"Three? How long are the classes?"

"An hour each. I go to the early morning ones on Saturday and Monday and then I'll take an evening class on Thursday nights." Then she gasped. "Damn! I missed Thursday's class because I covered for Martin."

Spencer hugged her closer and gave her a loud, smacking kiss. "I don't think you have to worry. Our romp in the dressing room was full of cardio."

Penny laughed out loud as she playfully smacked him. "I know I should be offended by that, but I can't be."

"Why?" he laughed. "Why be offended?"

"Because you sounded so smug!" But she kept on laughing and when their gazes met, she suddenly didn't feel like laughing any more. When she was able to catch her breath, she nibbled at her bottom lip. "You know…while that was a cardio workout, I don't think it can count as a good substitution for my class."

One of Spencer's brows arched at her. "No?"

She shook her head. "Zumba is an hour-long class," she explained. "Lots of dancing and moving and sweating."

"We certainly didn't dance," he said, his voice dropping slightly.

"We did move," she said softly, inching her lips toward his.

"And I know we sweat."

Penny couldn't contain the small smile that crossed her lips. "But if we're going to compete with Zumba, then we'd need to try…harder."

"I'm always up for a challenge," Spencer replied right before he closed the distance between them and kissed her.

Eventually this would stop, right? She asked herself. Eventually they'd get to a place where the physical need – the craving – would lessen. It had to. But right now, it wasn't. As she crawled over him and straddled his lap, all she could think about was how it had felt like far too long since they'd been together.

"Let's go upstairs," she said breathlessly against his lips.

"Done," he agreed as he stood with her in his arms and walked them up the stairs.

And hours later, Penny was fairly certain they had done the equivalent of two Zumba classes.

Now, fresh from her morning Zumba class Monday morning and on her way to Enchanted, she looked down as her phone rang. Assuming it was Spencer, she answered without looking at the screen.

"Hey," she said softly, almost purring.

"Um…Ms. Blake?"

Oh, crap! She thought. Not Spencer!

"Yes, this is Penny Blake," she said nervously.

"Ms. Blake, this is Derek Adams from Wells Fargo," he began, his tone serious and businesslike.

And it didn't give her a good feeling at all.

"Good morning, Mr. Adams," she replied,

willing the nervous tremor from her voice. "How are you today?"

"Fine, thank you," he responded. "Ms. Blake, after careful consideration, your request for a small business loan has been denied. We've sent a letter out to you with further explanation, but...I wanted to call you in person and let you know."

Right. Because hearing bad news was always easier when it was delivered twice, she thought miserably.

Her eyes immediately welled with tears and she swallowed hard before speaking again. "I appreciate you reaching out to me. I'll look for that letter in the mail. Thank you." And she hung up before he could offer some empty consolation. She was nobody to him and her business meant nothing to him.

"Dammit," she murmured, slamming her hand on the steering wheel. She wanted to cry – and probably would just as soon as she wasn't in the middle of traffic – but for right now she was angry. Really angry.

Why? Why did she even think she'd be able to pull this off? Having a business of her own and making it all happen like she'd dreamed? Who was she kidding? Letting out a shaky sigh, Penny maneuvered through the throng of cars on the road and saw her exit coming up. Getting over into the right-hand lane, she cursed again.

Why was it that good things seemed to happen for everyone she knew and not for her? Why was it like some unattainable dream for her to have it all? Just once! Things were going well with Spencer and up until three minutes ago, she really believed that there was still a chance for her to get her loan approved. But now…now she wasn't sure what she was going to do or what other options there were for her.

Or if she even wanted to look for them.

Right now, what she wanted was someone to tell her it was all going to be okay – that there were other banks she could go to – but she had a feeling that she'd just get the same answer.

And that was a completely depressing thought.

Looking at her phone she debated on whether to call Spencer and tell him what had happened, or maybe her parents, or maybe even Hailey.

But she didn't.

Taking her exit, she turned at the traffic light and began to look around almost frantically.

Pulling over at the first spot she could – a small shopping center only blocks away from Enchanted – she put the car in park and let out a shaky sigh just before she burst into tears.

SEVEN

Spencer grabbed his laptop and slid it into his bag, then checked his desk for anything else he was going to need for his weekend in Raleigh.

For a little more than a month, he and Penny had been making it work. After that first night when they talked about it, he had stayed through the following weekend. It wasn't ideal, and it turned out that she led a very busy life that left him on his own more than he had hoped. But when they got together at the end of the day and the few nights he got to sleep with her in his arms, it was all worth it.

And…he had been thankful that he'd been there on the day she was turned down for her small business loan. The look of utter devastation on her face when she opened the door to him would stay with him for a long time. She'd cried and he did everything he could to listen and be supportive, but she was hurting and there really wasn't anything he could do to make that better for her.

Apparently, her bosses had offered to be the ones to loan her the money to start her glam squad business, but Penny turned them down. She didn't want a handout and claimed that she knew the women already had plans for expansion and she didn't want to take anything away from them financially.

He loved and admired her pride even as it was keeping her from achieving her dream.

Since that day, Penny put on a brave face and claimed that maybe the timing just wasn't right and she'd revisit the idea eventually. At least, that's what she said at first. Then she started adding the word "maybe" to the end of that statement.

That's when he started to worry.

He looked around the office one more time as the alarm on his phone told him it was time to head to the airport. His Uber should be waiting downstairs.

Every time he flew up to be with her after that first week, he made sure to bring more work with him to keep him busy. So far, neither of his bosses minded him working remotely, but they were coming to a point in their current project that he was going to need to be more accessible and physically on site for meetings. It was something he was going to discuss with Penny this weekend.

He'd been afraid to mention it and didn't want to seem insensitive but maybe now that the plans for her business were temporarily on hold – and he firmly believed that – maybe she would consider coming to Atlanta for a week and seeing how he lived. Her work ethic was such that he knew she wouldn't want to leave Hailey in a lurch, but with enough advanced notice, she'd consider it.

Something to talk about this week.

The drive to the airport was uneventful and his flight took off on time. Spencer took that as a good sign. He didn't have to check any bags because he'd been leaving things at Penny's – and at his parents' – so he was able to walk right off the plane to where Penny was waiting for him in her car.

Their first night back together was always his favorite. He loved to see the smile on her face when he climbed into the car. Their first kiss was always the sweetest because he missed the taste of her all week long. They'd gotten into the habit of grabbing one form or another of takeout and eating at home and just enjoying the time to talk in person rather than on the phone.

As they walked through her front door with their arms loaded with pizza and a box of baked goods from the coffee shop at Enchanted, Spencer listened as she talked about the plans for the next evening's fashion show.

"Are you going to come and watch?" she asked. Normally he didn't go – mainly because it was about four hours of his time when he felt like he was just in the way – but this time…

"Actually, I am," he said and watched as her eyes lit up.

"Really?"

He nodded as he opened the pizza box. "Remember I told you about my friend Keith and getting invited to be part of his bridal party?"

She nodded.

"Turns out he and his fiancée are going to be at the show tomorrow night and I said I'd meet him there. He's going specifically to look at tuxedoes and I told him I was kind of a pro at that sort of thing so…"

Penny burst out laughing. "So you're a pro now?" she asked.

Grabbing a slice of pizza and putting it on Penny's plate before taking one for himself, he replied, "You know it. I've tried on quite a few and – if I do say so myself – I can tell the difference between a quality tux and a not-so-quality tux." He gave her a lecherous grin before adding, "I'm practically a professional groomsman."

That just had her laughing again. "I love that! Maybe we can get you a job with Martin on the weeks that you're in town."

"Let's not get carried away…"

"And you do realize that while you've tried on quite a few tuxes, you've yet to actually *be* a groomsman, right?"

"Technicalities…"

She laughed some more and it was good to see her finally relaxing a bit.

He took a bite of his dinner and chewed as he realized this was the perfect opening to talk to her about what he needed.

"I was wondering what you thought of maybe staying an extra day or two this time? Maybe we can take a trip to the coast and be beach bums for a couple of days. What do you think?" When he didn't answer right away, she put her slice down and studied him. "Spencer?"

He let out a sigh. "Okay, here's the thing..." And then he went on to explain to her all about his current project at work and all of the things that were going to happen from this point on and why he needed to be back in Atlanta more. Not sure what her reaction was going to be, Spencer tried to talk about all of the great things they could do if she came to see him and how he would make the time to show her around.

"Wow," she said when he was done. "I...I guess I've been a little selfish, huh?"

His eyes went wide. "What? Why would you even say that?"

Penny gave him a mild look. "Seriously? You've been doing all the traveling, all the compromising so that I'm not inconvenienced. That's not how it should be in a relationship, Spencer. We should be splitting the travel time fifty-fifty. If this is going to work..."

"It *is* working," he quickly corrected.

"But if it's going to *continue* to work...the travel has to be on each of us. I'm sorry that you've been doing it all. I guess...I guess I just figured you didn't mind it and that it gave you the opportunity to come home and see your family too. Two birds, one stone and all that."

And while she did have a point, the only thing he'd been getting out of his visits with his family was how much better they thought his life would be if he just moved home and took over his father's firm. He hadn't shared any of that with Penny because...well...

Shit.

He hadn't shared it because he didn't want her pressuring him too.

That didn't say much for how he was viewing this relationship if he was keeping something as important as this from her, did it?

"Okay, I have a confession to make," he said after a minute, and when she just looked at him with a curious expression, he went on. "I enjoy coming to Raleigh to see you and my family…"

"But…"

"But…seeing my family has kind of not been a good thing."

Penny immediately reached for his hand and squeezed it. "What's going on?"

"Remember when I told you about my father wanting me to take over his firm?"

She nodded.

"Well, the more time I spend here…"

"The more he's pushing for it," she finished for him.

"Exactly."

She sighed and reached for her drink and took a long sip. "So what have you been telling him?"

"Basically, I've been stalling – talking about the projects I'm already committed to and how I can't just quit my job."

"And how has he responded?"

Spencer shrugged. "He understands but then he talks about six months down the road or a year down the road…like if I just let my bosses know what's coming, they'll start to phase me out so I'll be able to leave when my work is done."

"And you still don't want that." It wasn't a

question. And he heard the sadness in her voice.

There was no way he could lie to her. "I...I don't," he finally said, his voice thick with emotion. It was the first time he admitted it out loud when he didn't feel good about it.

Placing her cup down on the coffee table, Penny leaned back against the sofa cushions. It took a minute before she would look at him. "I think we've hit that point where we need to re-address where we're going."

Dammit.

Not like this. He didn't want it to be like this or like anything. In his mind, they always found a way to make it work! Of course, in his mind it always involved Penny moving to Atlanta to be with him, but...

She sat up straight and took a steadying breath. "I think I should come to Atlanta and check it out."

Um...say what?

"Really?"

She nodded. "I think the timing is perfect. Obviously I'm not staring my own business – that's not going to happen – so there's nothing keeping me here."

"What about your family?"

She waved him off. "I told you how not everyone lives here anymore and my parents are plenty busy with their grandkids; they'll barely miss me."

He was beginning to notice a pattern here, and he didn't like it.

"What about your job? You love working for Enchanted," he argued lightly. "You talk about it all the time and it seems like you're really an integral part of the team."

Another wave. "Please, things are a little crazy right now because Ella just had her baby – a little boy, by the way – and I'm taking on more responsibility and all, but…"

Unable to help himself, Spencer reached for both of her hands and held them tightly. "Penny, it's okay to love your job. I get it. I respect that. I'm not asking you to give all that up."

Her eyes shone with tears just waiting to fall. "Look, I do love my job with Enchanted, but…it's just a job. I've done all that I can there. It's never going to be any more than what it is. And do I really want to be a salesgirl for the rest of my life?" She shrugged. "I don't know. But I can do that anywhere. I don't have to be here in Raleigh. I'm sure there are bridal shops in Atlanta too."

But there was no excitement in her words. No joy. And if there's one thing he always loved about listening to Penny talk, it was how she found joy in everything.

"Let's not worry about that now," he said because his mind was spinning in a million different directions and he needed to let all of this new information settle for a bit. "Tell me about tomorrow night's show and what I can do to help so that I'm not in the way."

And then she did smile.

And he knew he was in trouble.

"Penny? Can you fix Lisa's hair? We just switched out her veil..."

"Penny? When you're done with that can you help Tori with her makeup?"

"Penny? Do you happen to have any pink nail polish? Jenny has on black polish and..."

On and on it went as Penny ran around in that final hour before the show. She loved it. She loved the pace, the energy and then stepping back and seeing how great everyone looked. The only problem was that with all of her running around making everyone else beautiful, she wasn't ready.

Becca ran toward her and handed her a bottle of water and a giant cookie and smiled. "It may not be a great dinner, but you earned it tonight. I swear, it was like everyone had a problem with the simplest things!"

Penny readily agreed, took a large bite of the cookie and moaned with pleasure. "Damn, that's good."

Becca's smile grew. "Thanks. You looked like you needed a little something. I just gave one to Spencer too. He's been helping with the setup. It seems like we're a little short-handed everywhere tonight. We almost asked him to put on a tux and help out as one of the models."

Penny choked on the cookie. Becca patted her back until she caught her breath. "Um...what?"

"It turns out we didn't need to, but for a few minutes, we were down a groomsman. Turns out that Derek Mitchell was running late and forgot to call." Then she looked around. "We need to get you into your gown next."

Nodding, she took another bite of the chocolate chip cookie and a swig of water before heading toward her dressing room. Together, she and Becca worked to get her into the gown and secure her headpiece. "We really should think about eliminating the headpieces for the show," she said.

"How come?"

"For ease of getting the girls changed faster. It's easier to do a hairstyle that will go with everything than to have to fix and adjust after every dress change. It might make for less confusion. Plus, I think sometimes the veil can distract from the dress and someone might count out a gown because of how it looks with the headpiece."

Becca considered her for a moment. "I think that makes total sense. We'll bring that up Monday at the meeting."

Once she was dressed, she studied her reflection in the mirror and smiled.

This is my dress, she thought and gasped.

"What? What's the matter? Are you okay?" Becca asked nervously.

"No...no. It's...it's nothing. This gown is just..."

"It's perfect for you," Becca finished. "You wore a similar one about a month ago that we all talked about because of the silvery blue hue to it. This one has it too and it just...it compliments you in every way."

She sighed longingly. "If only..."

"Oh, come on. Someday you'll be wearing it as your own. Things seem like they're going really well with Spencer."

"They are," she agreed, "but…I'm never going to have a big wedding."

"What?" Becca cried. "Why not?"

"I'm the youngest of nine kids. My parents helped pay for everyone else's weddings but…they've already kind of let me know that the well is dry where that's concerned. There's so many grandkids now and they want to retire and…" She shrugged. "I'd be on my own to pay for it."

"Not completely alone…"

"You know what I mean," Penny said wearily. "I need to get out of debt and that's not going to happen if I have to pay for a big wedding."

"You don't necessarily need a big wedding to have a fabulous gown," Becca countered. "Ella and Dylan had a very small and intimate wedding and she wore a fantastic gown – similar to this one – and it was great."

Another shrug. "Maybe. But…I just don't see that in my future."

"Not even for Spencer?"

Ugh…she didn't want to think about that right now. Things were already heading in a direction that she didn't love but…she loved him so…

"Penny!" Hailey called out. "We're almost ready for you! You ready?"

As I'll ever be…

Two hours later, Penny was walking around the banquet room talking to potential clients and wearing the gown she had worn on her first round of the show.

Her gown.

"There you are," Spencer said from behind her and her heart actually kicked hard in her chest.

There was no way he would know how she felt about this dress, and him, and all the scenarios in her mind for how she wished he was seeing her in it. Turning, she smiled. "Here I am!"

He was standing with a couple she assumed to be his friend Keith and his fiancée – which Spencer immediately confirmed as he introduced them. They chatted for a few minutes and Penny almost melted when Spencer came to stand beside her and wrapped his arm around her waist. Then he nuzzled her ear as he whispered, "You look beautiful."

Um, yeah…it was a good thing he had an arm around her because she was pretty sure her knees were ready to buckle.

"Thank you," she said softly. "I heard you were quite the hero here tonight."

He looked at her in confusion.

"Becca mentioned how you helped out just about everywhere."

"Well," he said with a hint of bashfulness. "I was just standing around and it seemed like they could use a hand."

"She also mentioned how they almost asked you to be a groomsman in the show tonight." She said it lightly and enjoyed the look of mild panic on his face.

"Um…say what now? No one said anything about…" Then he stopped. "Wait, why didn't they ask me? Because – if you think about it – I've tried on enough of those tuxedos that I could totally get up on stage and model one."

She couldn't help but laugh. "You did mention how you were practically a pro at it now," she said with a sassy wink. Before she could say anything more, Hailey was waving her over to show her gown to a prospective client. "I'm sorry but…I need to go. It was nice meeting you both."

Before she could walk away, Spencer held her hand and faced her. "I know you still have some time to put in here, but do you want to get something to eat when you're done?"

"I do."

Oh God…had she just said "I do" while wearing a wedding gown and facing Spencer? Again?'

His knowing smirk told her he caught her Freudian slip. Then he leaned forward and kissed her forehead. "Go and show off your gown…"

"My gown?" she squeaked. "It's not…I mean…it's not *my* gown…per se…I mean…"

Spencer chuckled. "You know what I mean," he said as he gently turned her in Hailey's direction. "Go and do your thing and I'll be waiting for you when you're done."

Penny looked at him over her shoulder as she walked away and all she could think of was how much she wanted to be with him – near him. This long-distance thing wasn't working for her anymore. She knew what she wanted and knew she was going to do whatever it took to have it.

❧

"Hey, Spencer," Angie said as she walked over. "Thanks for helping out earlier with the setup."

"My pleasure."

"So um…would you mind giving me a hand moving some of these chairs back? We're still a little short-handed and I hate the thought of leaving all of this out."

"No problem." There were a hundred chairs lined up on either side of the runway and he and Angie worked on one side, while the few members of their usual breakdown crew managed the other. "Can I ask you a question?"

"Sure."

"Why don't you just leave all of this set up? You do enough of these shows so I would imagine it would save a lot of time to just leave the chairs out."

She didn't even blink as she picked up a couple of chairs and went to stack them. "Each show is a little bit different. We like to try new things and it's easier to come in here and figure out what we want to do if the room is clear."

He nodded in understanding and went about stacking his own section of chairs.

"How long are you in town for?" she asked.

"Just until Tuesday." Then he gave a brief rundown of the work waiting for him back in Atlanta. "This will probably be the last show I see for a while."

"Damn. I know Penny's going to be disappointed. She was really excited about you being here tonight."

He was maneuvering a stack of chairs when Becca came over to help. After a quick hello to him, she started talking to Angie. "Have you seen Penny?"

"She's in the back getting changed. How come?" Angie replied.

"Hailey's talking with a large bridal party right now that wants to hire Penny to do her whole glam squad treatment on them. I thought she'd want to know."

"Wow! That's awesome!" Angie said excitedly. "Now would be the perfect time for her to have a studio. I hate how that didn't work out. Damn bank."

"I know," Becca said. "Oh, and check this out - we were talking earlier, and she had some great ideas on how to make show prep a little easier on everyone and I told her we'd talk about it on Monday but I figured I'd share it with you in case I forget."

"I swear, I think we've all been doing this for so long that we don't ever think about changing anything. It's great how Penny sees ways to make improvements that we don't."

Spencer didn't want to chime in, but he was kind of curious about a few things…

Putting the chairs down, he stepped over to the women. "Can I ask you both something?"

"Sure," they replied.

"Um…if what Penny wants to do is going to be such an asset to this place – to Enchanted," he specified, "why not pay for it yourselves, set it up and let Penny rent it and run it? You know she has the talent to carry it. Why does she have to own it outright?"

Becca looked a little uncomfortable and Angie looked mildly annoyed.

"I mean no disrespect," he said quickly. "It just seems that for all that Penny contributes to the business…"

"Penny has been a lifesaver," Becca said. "Honestly, I don't know how we could have handled some of the more difficult things without her. She lends a hand wherever she's needed and honestly, she's wonderful with the customers. She has great insights and she's basically like a jack-of-all-trades in the wedding world."

"I know that," Spencer replied, happy that others appreciated all of the hard work Penny did. "I just don't understand why there isn't anything being done to let her do what she's most passionate about. Just because the bank turned her down doesn't mean there aren't other alternatives."

Angie was still glaring at him a little and Spencer almost excused himself when she finally spoke. "We offered to lend her the money," Angie began calmly, "and she turned us down."

"She knows how you've already got expansion plans in the works…"

"Yeah, yeah, yeah," Angie interrupted. "That's what she said to us too and we respect that. Most of our plans aren't going to go into effect for at least a year or two down the road. All of this?" She motioned to the space around them. "This is all brand-freaking-new. Believe me, we're not looking to lay out any more money right now, but we would have to help Penny. We can't force her to take the money."

He knew that, he really did, but he also knew how much he hated to see her disappointed and upset. Yesterday, she had talked about being okay with walking away from this job and these people, but watching her in action tonight told a completely different story.

"And I don't see why you're not over the moon at this whole thing," Angie said, snapping him out of his thoughts.

"How so?"

"With the business off the table, no doubt she'd be more open to going with you to Atlanta," she said with just a hint of malice. "If anything, I would think you'd be sending a basket of muffins to the bank as a thank you."

"Angie…" Becca warned.

"It's true! He's got everything to gain here! No more flying back and forth. No more crazy schedules for him to keep up with, and Penny can move and play house with him so he can keep his job and stop being inconvenienced."

"Hey!" he snapped. "I never said any of those things!"

She leaned in close. "You didn't have to. Believe it or not, I've been in the same spot you and Penny are. My husband used to live up in New York and I was here. His job prevented him from moving and I had to make a choice. I chose him."

"A little begrudgingly," Becca mumbled.

"Shut up," Angie said, but there was no heat behind her words. "Anyway, I left here – the only place I had ever known and all my friends and my job – and moved up to New York."

"For a few weeks," Becca said quickly as she looked the other way.

"Oh, for the love of it, Becca! I'm trying to make a point here!"

"Then make it already!" Becca cried. "Sheesh!"

"I moved and I would have stayed – I would have found a way to make it work – but I wasn't happy. Sean knew it even though I denied it. We got lucky – his job allowed him to make the move and work remotely with a little bit of travel. Once we talked about it and knew that it would only be like that for a short amount of time, we knew the right thing to do was to come back here. Mrs. J – Hailey's mom and the original owner of Enchanted – she even offered me a job here when she thought I was going to be staying in New York."

"Why did you move if you really didn't want to?" Spencer asked. "Wouldn't telling Sean how miserable you were about the whole thing make a lot more sense?"

She huffed with annoyance. "Actually, I did tell him, and we broke up and he went back to New York and I stayed here. Then I realized that I loved him enough to try to make it work."

It was on the tip of his tongue to remind her that obviously she didn't try all that hard since they came back but…he didn't.

"In the end, we talked more about it and figured out a plan that worked for us both. And now we're here and we're both happy."

There was a bit of an accusatory tone that caught him off guard. What exactly had Penny been sharing with them?

"All I want is for Penny to be happy," he began cautiously. "And I have not in any way tried to convince her to move to Atlanta with me. I've asked her to come and visit – maybe come for a weekend to see how I live just like I've been doing by coming here – but she's been turning me down because of the job. At least…she had been…"

"Oh my God!" Angie said with exasperation. "Are you seriously standing here right now telling us that she's going to quit?"

"What?! No!" he said defensively. "I didn't say that at all! I'm just saying that when I got here yesterday she was a little more open to asking for some time off to come see me!"

His heart was racing and he felt a little like he was under the shining light of an interrogation. Where were all these accusations coming from and how did this suddenly become about him?

With a steadying breath, he held up his hands to halt any further comments. "Look, Penny and I are trying to figure things out. As you obviously know, long-distance relationships are not ideal. On top of the stress from that, I hate seeing Penny upset about the business and having her plans fall through. It's her dream and she's really good at it and I just was hoping to find a way for her to have it. All I want – all I've ever wanted – is for her to be happy."

"Aww," Becca said with a small smile. "That is so sweet."

Angie glared at him. "Mmm...maybe," she grumbled. "Just remember that when you're trying to get your way all the way in Atlanta."

"What about Atlanta?"

They all turned at the sound of Penny's voice. She had changed back into her casual clothes and her hair was up in a long ponytail. She looked happy and relaxed and...totally in her element.

Before he could say anything, she launched into a conversation with the girls about some of the gowns from the show and who was coming in tomorrow for them and then Becca started talking about the bridal party who was in need of Penny's glam squad services and Spencer excused himself quietly and went back to moving chairs.

He had a feeling they were going to be talking for a while.

EIGHT

Something was up. She'd been saying it for days but as Spencer left Tuesday morning, her suspicion grew. He'd been a little distant after the show Friday night and even though they had a great weekend, it wasn't hard to tell that he had something on his mind. It could have been work that was distracting him, but for some reason, she didn't think so. At her meeting on Monday she had tried to feel out Becca and Angie about it – being that she had found them all talking together after the show, but they didn't seem to have anything to share either.

Weird.

Penny wasn't one to make waves or force anyone to talk about things they didn't want to talk about, so she tried to push it out of her mind. She had asked for a four-day weekend off as soon as it could be arranged so she could go to Atlanta and Hailey had been more than accommodating. Well, as accommodating as she could be when Ella was out on maternity leave and they had shows scheduled.

All she had to do was wait three weeks.

While that might not seem like a lot, Penny knew Spencer had spoiled her. She was used to seeing him more often and it was going to be hard to deal with only seeing each other via FaceTime or Skype.

As they were closing up the shop for the night, it was down to just Penny and Hailey.

"I don't know about you, but that last bride just about wore me out," Hailey said as she sat down at her desk.

"I agree. It was almost as if she'd never even looked at wedding gowns before. I don't think I've ever met a bride who didn't have some idea of what she wanted."

Hailey rubbed at her temples. "Hey, um…Jack's working late tonight and I was going to go grab some sushi. Want to join me?"

For a moment, Penny was a little dumbstruck. As much as she and her bosses got along and spent time together, it was normally all work-related. She'd never gone out socially with any of them.

"Um…sure," she agreed.

Within minutes, the shop was closed and they were both in Hailey's BMW, driving to her favorite sushi restaurant. The conversation was fairly neutral – today's clients and what was on the schedule for tomorrow – and Penny felt herself relaxing. Not that she wanted to only talk about work, but it was a topic she felt comfortable talking to Hailey about.

It wasn't until they were seated and had ordered that Hailey brought up the glam squad.

"So, what are your plans for your business?" she asked.

For a minute, Penny wasn't sure what to say. "Well…um…nothing. I need to work on paying off the last of my student loans and getting my credit in a little better shape before I can even think of doing anything."

"I know you turned down our offer for help – and I totally respect your reasons – but I hate to think of you not moving forward with it, Penny. Your plan was spot on and I can envision the salon so clearly that it's killing me that it's not going to be there." She paused and gave her a sympathetic smile. "Have you thought about asking your parents for the money?"

Just as she had explained to Becca on Friday night, she told Hailey all about her family and their situation. "Honestly, if I can't get them on board to potentially help pay for my wedding – should I ever get married – how can I possibly think they'll be able to help with money for a business?"

"Well, for starters, this is something you'd be paying back. You aren't asking for the money free and clear, right?"

"No, but…"

"And it would show that you're taking initiative to be an independent and responsible adult and business owner – one who could make enough money to pay for her own dream wedding when the time came," Hailey went on.

"Maybe, but…"

"And you can draw up a contract with them so they know you're serious about paying them back or maybe offer them some sort of share of the business. I know I'd be happy to sit down with them – as would my mom and the girls – and tell them how much we support the business and everything we'd do to help it grow."

Penny's head was spinning. She was so certain that this wasn't going to happen and had resigned herself to it and to picking up and moving to Atlanta to be with Spencer that…

Spencer!

She must have gasped or said his name because Hailey reached across the table, concern written all over her face. "Penny? Are you okay?"

Was she?

At the moment, the answer was definitely no.

If anything, her heart was racing and she felt like she was hyperventilating. Hailey immediately walked around the table to her and forced her to have something to drink as she tried to calm her down. By the time she did, she was mildly embarrassed.

"Sorry."

As she sat back down, Hailey smiled. "Don't be. Are you sure you're okay?"

Penny nodded but…right now, she needed…

"Can I ask you something?" she asked quickly before she lost her nerve.

"Of course. Anything," Hailey replied.

"But I need you to be like…a friend and not my boss," she said hesitantly.

And then Hailey gave her a reassuring smile. "Penny, I would have thought by now that you would consider me a friend."

"I do, I really do, but…you're also my boss and this kind of has to do with work so…"

Hailey held up a hand to stop her. "Okay. Got it. No boss here. Just two friends out for sushi."

And then Penny poured her heart out – about Spencer, about how she was thinking of moving to Atlanta and how she was torn about the entire thing.

When she was done, Hailey didn't say anything right away and then their food arrived so that was a distraction. It wasn't until they had each taken a few bites when Hailey put her chopsticks down and spoke.

"I know I said no boss here, but for a minute or two, I might be."

Penny nodded.

"I think I can speak for everyone at Enchanted when I say that the thought of losing you is just awful. You never were just an employee, Penny. You were one of the girls – family. That being said, I understand exactly what you're saying and how you feel. You have this opportunity to be with an amazing man who you've been in love with since forever. The two of you have waited so long for things to go your way and it sucks that work – for the both of you – is such an obstacle."

Then Penny explained about Spencer's father and the opportunity he has at the firm.

"But that's not what he wants," Hailey said, and Penny shook her head. "Then it's not an option to even take into consideration."

"I know, I know but…it would be so great if…"

"You can't think that way. Because it might not seem like a big deal now, but eventually it will be. Then not only will there be tension between the two of you, but tension between Spencer and his family. And that's not going to help the situation."

Damn, she hadn't thought of it like that.

"So what do I do? What if I give up my job and move and end up miserable down in Atlanta? What if I can't find work or I end up with a job I hate? Isn't that the same thing?"

Hailey studied her for a minute. "There is that possibility, but you could also find something wonderful that you'll love. And believe me, as supportive as I'm trying to be, the selfish part of me hates saying it!" They both laughed softly. "You know what I'm saying. Spencer already knows he's going to be miserable working with his father, whereas you have the opportunity to find something that works for you."

"I don't know. I think that's going to be hard to find no matter what. Even now."

"What do you mean?"

She let out a breath and figured she might as well be totally – even brutally – honest. "I'm not happy right now," she said. "I'm disappointed about my business getting rejected by the bank and I feel like I'm at a standstill. I enjoy doing the work with you in the bridal shop, but subbing all over the place is just starting to…well, it's getting…"

"You hate it," Hailey finished for her but there was no condemnation in her words. "I get it.

Personally, I wouldn't like it much either. And after all of the things you shared with me about Martin and how he's running the tuxedo shop, we've had a long and drawn-out meeting with him to explain to him our expectations and how he needs to step up his game. We can't have groomsmen coming in and feeling like they're not being taken care of or being taken care of poorly."

"Oh, well…that's good. I guess."

"I'm sorry if we took advantage of your willingness to help out. That wasn't fair of us."

Penny shrugged and gave her a weak smile. "For a while I didn't mind it. But now? Now I think everything is going to be a disappointment because…well, because I'm disappointed. I know I'll get over it eventually, but right now I think I might just need a change."

"I see."

They finished their meal in relative silence before Hailey picked up the check. After she handed her card to the waitress, she looked at Penny.

"I am going to support you no matter what you decide. I want you to know that. And I'm going to help you with whatever it is that you need. If you go to Atlanta and hate it and want to move back, there will always be a position for you with Enchanted."

"Thank you."

"Just one more thing, I want you to promise that you'll come and talk to me and let me know what you decide or even if you just need someone to vent to. I'm always here."

"I appreciate that."

❧❧

"So you were back in the tux shop? Even after Hailey talked to Martin?" Spencer asked a week later.

"Yup," she sighed. "I don't think his heart is in the business and to be honest, it's killing me to sit back and watch him ruin it. It's just so wrong how someone like him can have a business and doesn't appreciate it, while I have all these ideas for a place of my own and I'm not allowed to have one!" She growled in frustration. "There is so much potential there!" She began to talk about promotional ideas and ways to fix up the shop and – again – there was an excitement in her voice that wasn't there a whole lot lately.

Especially whenever she talked about moving to Atlanta.

"Have you given any more thought to talking to your folks about helping you with the business?" he asked.

She let out a long breath. "You know, as much as I want to, I just can't. You have no idea how many times I've thought about it."

"But…?"

"But then I remember how they told me about wanting to retire and all the ways they've helped my siblings and…I don't know…I think I was just born too late."

"Oh, Penny. You can't think like that."

"But it's true," she said sadly. "They already

put eight kids through school, helped pay for weddings, welcomed a dozen grandkids – give or take – and I think they're just done."

"That's not fair," he argued lightly. "You're their child too. Just because you were born last doesn't mean you don't deserve the same help they gave their other kids."

"You don't understand."

On that, she was right. He didn't. Not that he had any idea what it was like to come from such a large family, but how was it fair that Penny had to be the one singled out not to get the help her siblings had?

"Maybe you should do as Hailey suggested and bring them in to talk to her and the girls? Maybe if they saw the potential, they wouldn't look at this as a financial strain, you know?"

She was silent for a moment. "All my life I was fine with hand-me-downs and not having all the things my oldest siblings had. But I had something none of them had – once everyone moved out, I had Mom and Dad to myself for a little while. With no one to share the attention, it was just the three of us and it was awesome."

He could hear the joy in her voice and it made him smile.

"They've done so much for all of their kids and really, what right do I have to stand there and demand more of them? How crappy would that be?"

"I wouldn't call it crappy…"

"You know what I'm saying, Spencer. I love my parents and I'm thankful for all that they've done for me. And besides, if I had to ask them for anything, it wouldn't be for a business, it would be for a…" Her words cut short before she quickly added, "It's nothing. Either way, I'm not going to involve them in this."

"But Penny…"

"Ugh…enough about me," she quickly interrupted, "let's talk about you. How's work going? Everything on track with this project?"

He'd been sharing his work schedule with her, as well as the building schedule and how much of a struggle it is to keep on track when dealing with subcontractors and waiting on permits. "For the most part," he replied. "I got an assistant assigned to me to help with a lot of the legwork so that I can focus on the bigger engineering issues and be in my office."

"Oh…well…that's good, right?"

"I don't know. I kind of enjoy being on site. I'm always fascinated when we break ground and when I can watch things progress in person."

"You can still go to the site though, right?"

"Oh, yeah. Definitely. But I feel like I've been relegated to my office and someone else is getting to have all the fun."

She laughed softly and he loved the sound of it.

"Either way, it's temporary and my bosses are already looking at the next project for me to work on."

"Oh, wow. That's kind of fast. I would think you'd only work on one project at a time."

"Normally that's the case, but there are some new jobs we're bidding on that I expressed an interest in so…"

This was one of the nights that they were simply on the phone rather than using FaceTime or Skype and right now he wished he could see her face.

"It sounds like you're going to be pretty busy for a while," she said softly. "If it's not a good time to come down…"

"Are you kidding me? I can't wait to see you," he said earnestly. "I miss you, Penny. I can't wait for you to get here so I can show you around and have you here in my home for a change." Then he looked around and realized he'd better do something to spruce it up a bit before she arrived.

"I miss you too."

After they hung up, Spencer spent a lot of time sitting on the sofa, lost in thought. Besides sprucing up the place so that she wouldn't be disappointed in it, he knew he'd also have to wrap up a lot of loose ends at work so they could actually spend time together and he could show her around. He still had well over a week to make that happen, but it wouldn't hurt to start burning the midnight oil now to make sure he stayed a little ahead.

Sitting up, he reached for his laptop and was just getting ready to look over some reports when his phone rang again.

His father.

Shit.

"Hey, Dad," he said pleasantly.

"Hey, Spencer. I didn't catch you at a bad time, did I?"

"No, not at all. I was just…relaxing," he lied.

"What's up?"

"Well, I was a little hesitant to call you because you've been pretty vocal about the offer to come and work for me, but…"

"What's going on, Dad?" There was something in his father's voice that wasn't sitting well with him.

"I've been approached by a large design firm. They'd like to buy me out and take over – use what I've built here over the years to expand their own company."

Holy. Crap. "Really? That's…that's great, Dad. How do you feel about it?"

"Honestly, I don't know. I was hoping you'd have some advice."

That was surprising. "Me? What kind of advice could I possibly give? I think this would allow you to retire comfortably – more so than you would if I were to come in and take over for you. You would probably have time to help work with the transition so it's not like you'd be out right away…"

His father laughed softly. "You realize that was advice you just gave me, right?"

Spencer laughed with him. "I guess so." He paused. "But how do you feel about it? I mean…this is your company, your baby. I know you're disappointed that it wasn't something I wanted to do, but…"

"Spencer, I think you wanted to do it, but I made it too unappealing to you."

Well…shit. "That's not true, Dad. Not really."

His father laughed again. "Believe it or not, I

wouldn't have wanted to work with my dad either."

"Grandpa was a lawyer. Of course you didn't want to work with him."

"That's not what I meant. It's not easy to be expected to follow in somebody's footsteps. There's a lot of pressure there, a lot of expectations and I realize now that you had your own vision for what you wanted to do and I was trying to make you conform to what I had built. I was closed-minded about what you saw for the firm's future and for that I'm sorry."

Raking a hand through his hair, Spencer let out a long breath. "You don't have to apologize, Dad. Like I said, this is your firm, your baby, so of course you didn't want to see it change."

"But it's going to anyway," he said wearily. "And I know it's a good thing, but…part of me is just a little sad about it."

And Spencer could understand that. "When is all this happening?"

"The proposal just came to me yesterday. I've been sitting here weighing the pros and cons and talking with my team to see if it was something they were on board with and…"

"And are they? Is anyone opposed to it?"

"Surprisingly, no. So many of my employees have been with me since the beginning and – like me – they're going to be retiring soon or hoping too. The younger architects and designers? They'll fit right in because I think I've held them back creativity-wise."

"I'm sure that's not true."

"Believe what you want," his father said with a

trace of amusement, "but you're not the only one I've been butting heads with."

Unfortunately, he did believe it, but he was trying to be nice. "I'm sorry I let you down, Dad. I feel like if I could have just..."

"Bit the bullet?" his father teased. "That's not what I wanted for you, Spencer. You should do what makes you happy. I have for forty years and I don't regret it. It wasn't always easy and the climb to have something of my own was hard, but I always loved my job. It made it possible for me to give my kids a good life and to spend time with your beautiful mother."

"Speaking of...how does Mom feel about all of this?"

"She's begging me to sign the papers now so that as soon as your sister's wedding is over, we can leave on a European vacation of some sort. She's dying to go to Italy and I have to admit, the chance to explore the architecture there is very appealing."

"Then you should do it. You only have another month until the wedding is over so..." His father was silent for so long that Spencer thought they'd lost the connection. "Dad? You still there?"

"I am," he said quietly. "It just struck me that in a month my baby girl will be married and moving out." Then he laughed. "Finally. And I'll be looking at retirement. That's a lot of change for me – a guy who doesn't like change."

Spencer knew that feeling exactly. He liked stability. Knowing what was coming. His schedule. It was all very...

Boring.

It was very boring.

He thought of Penny and her ever-changing schedule – the way she always went with the flow with a smile on her face and had stories of the things she learned or experienced from taking a different path once in a while. Other than her negative interactions with Martin, she took everything in stride and he loved hearing her stories.

She didn't have stability; she had experiences.

She didn't have a schedule; she had dreams.

A slow smile crossed his face.

"Yeah, but…sometimes those changes take us to places that make us even happier than we ever thought possible."

৵৶৵

When Penny stepped out of the Atlanta airport, she sighed. It was far more crowded than the Raleigh one.

As they drove through downtown to Spencer's condo, she noted how much traffic there was and how congested it felt compared to home.

Stop doing that, she chided herself. *It's not supposed to be the same. It's okay for it to be different.*

"I thought about doing like we always do when we're in Raleigh and stopping for takeout on the way home, but I thought we'd bring your stuff to my place and then go out to eat. How does that sound?"

She smiled. "Sounds like a plan."

Ugh…could she sound any less enthused?

When they arrived at Spencer's condo she was…shocked. It was huge but it was…stark. Bare. Void of any personality. White walls, black furniture, stainless steel appliances…definitely not her style at all. He showed her around and it wasn't until they got to his bedroom that she saw any signs of the man she loved.

In the large room was a king-sized bed, a mountain of pillows and floor to ceiling windows that looked out on the city. He had a picture of the two of them next to his bed and when she saw it, she turned to him and smiled.

"I like looking at your face before I go to bed," he said as he came to stand beside her.

"We don't have any dinner reservations, do we?" she asked, turning toward him and reaching for his hands.

Spencer shook his head. "I figured we'd decide when you got here what we were in the mood for."

Best lead-in ever.

"I'm not in the mood for food," she said, pressing closer. "As a matter of fact, food is the furthest thing from my mind right now."

Without another word, Spencer lowered his head and claimed her lips with his.

Thank God, she thought. Three weeks was far too long. She clung to him, releasing his hands so that she could touch and be touched.

And boy did he touch.

Her hands raked up into his hair as Spencer reached down and squeezed her ass. She'd missed those hands, the feel of him, the heat of him…

Just…him.

"Too long," she murmured when he lifted his head to nip at her ear. His warm breath on her skin felt delicious and she was practically vibrating with need. Not that she wasn't primed for this – three weeks away from each other already had her on edge and then to take all of that pent-up energy and put them within a foot of a bed and she was ready to come undone.

"Yes," he said breathlessly as he tried to taste and touch her everywhere. "Too damn long."

Within minutes, Spencer had her stripped down to her panties and carefully guided her down to the bed. She lay back and watched as he tugged his shirt over his head and quickly discarded his shoes, socks and jeans. He stood before her in nothing but his briefs and she couldn't wait to touch him. Reaching out a hand to him, she gently tugged him onto the bed to cover her.

And then it was as if the universe righted itself.

All of the sadness and frustration and disappointment vanished as they pressed skin to skin and he kissed her – long and wet and deep and exactly how she liked it. Limbs tangled, breath mingled and rather than the frantic rush she thought they were building, everything slowed. Hands that were grabbing, now caressed, untamed kisses now seduced. It was the sweetest of reunions and they sank into it – getting reacquainted with each other.

And hopefully, this would be one of the last times they had to worry about being apart again.

❧❧

"I swear we'll go out to dinner tomorrow night, but this is exactly what I wanted tonight."

Beside her, Spencer laughed softly. "I have to agree. All week I've been obsessing about where I wanted to take you, but this is damn near perfect."

They were sprawled out on his sofa watching a movie on Netflix while enjoying takeout Chinese.

"I seriously think we need to just come to grips with the fact that this is our thing," Penny said, shaking a chopstick at him. "We talk a good game about being the type of people who enjoy going out to fancy restaurants, but at the end of the day, there is just something about being comfortable on the couch and eating some lo mein."

"Well, there are some merits to going out to a fancy restaurant…"

She shook her head. "Shoes, a bra, possibly some Spanx…too much work. This is much better."

"Believe me, I have no objections to you not wearing a bra," he teased. "Any time you want to stop wearing one, I'll support you one hundred percent."

She burst out laughing and had to put her carton of food down. "Support? Bra? Good one!"

When he realized what he'd said, he couldn't help but laugh with her. "Bad choice of words…" he said as he reached out and pulled her against him and kissed her senseless. "But a good visual." Then he was cupping her breasts and dinner was all but forgotten for a little while.

They resurfaced later to reheat their food and

opted to sit at the kitchen table to ensure they would eat.

"I swear I could eat another pint or two of this," Penny said as she picked up more noodles. "Too bad we couldn't have ice cream delivered."

"One step ahead of you," he said around a mouthful of Moo Shu. "I stocked up already. I made sure I got all of your favorites."

"Careful...you're spoiling me. At this rate I'm going to expect you to keep the freezer fully stocked even when I move here."

He choked on his dinner and it took a minute for him to catch his breath. "Are you serious? You...you're really going to move here?"

She nodded and gave him a bright smile.

Or what she hoped was a bright smile.

"I talked to Hailey and the girls before I left and told them that my mind was made up," she said with a curt nod. Then she reached for one of his hands and held it tightly. "I missed you so much these last few weeks and with so much time on my hands, I was able to think about things – about us – and I know that I don't want to do this long-distance thing anymore."

"But...what about your job? You love it at Enchanted," he countered.

She willed herself not to cry. Telling Hailey and Angie and Becca and even Ella – who happened to stop in with baby Devin – had been the hardest thing she'd ever done. Even telling her parents of her plans hadn't caused such a gut-wrenching reaction as watching the look on her bosses faces.

"I do...I mean, I did," she quickly corrected. "But things have changed and I'm ready to move on. Try something new. And if I stay in Raleigh, I'm never going to want to leave Enchanted. I'll always find a reason to stay. I love the girls and they're really more like friends than bosses...and I'm sure it won't be easy to find that kind of dynamic again. It's not completely unheard of but...I don't know...I'm sure there are bridal shops here that I can apply to and I'll make new friends. I mean, maybe not with my bosses but...that's okay, right? Are you friends with your bosses?"

He didn't get a chance to answer before she was talking again.

"Who knows...maybe I won't look at bridal shops. And maybe that would be okay...I mean, I enjoy what I do, and I know I'm good at it, but...it might be weird. I would almost feel like I'm competing against Enchanted even though we're six hours away. Maybe I'll apply at some salons and start doing hair again full-time. I can rent a booth or something to get started. Of course, in the beginning you need to build your client base so I'll only get the walk-ins or the people no one wants, and I'll have to see about getting my license here, but...I'm sure it will be fine." She sighed. "It's just time for a change."

Spencer wanted so badly to believe her and if she hadn't sounded so unsure or if she hadn't kept correcting herself he might have.

There wasn't anything he could say right now. There was too much to think about and to take into consideration. They only had the weekend together and he didn't want to spend it making her upset.

Which she clearly was.

A change of subject was in order and he did just that.

"So what flavor of ice cream are we starting with tonight?"

NINE

"I hate goodbyes."

"Me too."

Penny took a shaky breath and slowly let it out. "Not too much longer though, right? Soon we're going to be done with this."

Spencer nodded. "That's right. All this back and forth will be over before you know it."

She looked at him and put on a brave face. "I hope so." Then she hugged him. "I wish I could stay longer."

He held her tightly and kissed the top of her head. "You'd be bored. I'm swamped this week."

"I could have spent the time getting acquainted with the city and looking for a job." She looked at their joined hands. "I was thinking more about it, and I'll probably go back to doing hair. It will be easier to get started as long as I can transfer my license. There were a ton of salons that I saw when we were walking around downtown yesterday. I'm going to work on my resume and portfolio and hopefully I'll get into one of the more upscale salons – better tips – rather than one of the chain ones. Although, beggars can't be choosers, right?"

Rather than comment, he pulled back and looked at the line of people heading toward the security checkpoint. "I think you need to join the masses or you'll never get through in time."

Looking over her shoulder, she studied the line and sighed. "It's never like this in Raleigh," she murmured.

Hiding his smile, he pulled her in close again and kissed her. "It will all be okay. Text me when you land and call me when you get home, okay?"

She hugged him tightly. "What if I just stayed? Then when you have time off we'll go back to Raleigh together and we can just pack up my stuff. What do you think?"

Spencer laughed softly. "I think you're trying to find ways to avoid this security line."

"It's a really long line."

"I think you'll survive," he teased and cupped her face in his hands. "Go and I will talk to you when you get home."

She pouted slightly but did take a step away from him. "Fine. But if I miss my flight because this line took forever to get through, you're going to have to come back and get me."

"And you know I would."

Shoulders slumped, she finally gave up. "I'll text you when I land."

"And I want you to call me when you get home."

Nodding, she reached up and kissed him one last time. "When are you coming back to Raleigh?"

He laughed again. "Penny, we've been over this. I'll be there in two weeks. I promise."

She sighed again. "Okay. I guess I'll just talk to you later." Her eyes were already bright with unshed tears and she was killing him.

"Hey," he said softly before she turned away. Then he stepped in close, caressed her cheek. "This isn't forever. We can hang on for two weeks, right?"

Silently, she nodded.

Studying her face, feeling the softness of her skin, he rested his forehead against hers. "I love you."

She nodded again. "I love you too."

And then she quickly turned and walked away – probably unaware that it was the first time they had ever said that to each other.

As promised, Penny texted Spencer once the plane was at the gate and then called him when she got home. The call went to voicemail and she shrugged it off and figured that he was on another call – probably work-related. And while she was sad that they didn't get to talk, there really wasn't much to talk about. Her flight was only ninety-minutes long and even with the wait in line to get through security and her drive home when she landed, it had only been a few hours since they'd seen each other. The only thing she possibly had to talk about was the latest celebrity gossip she'd read about on the plane.

It was too early for dinner and she wasn't sure what to do with herself. Pulling out her phone she quickly checked the class schedule at the gym and opted to go for a Zumba class since she missed her usual one this morning. Julianne – her regular instructor – wasn't leading this one, but at least she'd get a workout in.

That was something else she was going to have to do – find a gym that offered Zumba in Atlanta.

By the time she got home later, she was exhausted. She'd stopped at the supermarket and picked up some groceries so she could make herself something to eat, and while she chopped up vegetables for her salad, she called Spencer again.

Voicemail.

"He works too damn hard," she murmured, adding slices of grilled chicken to her salad. With nothing left to do, Penny opted to eat her salad while watching TV. Hopefully by the time she was done, Spencer would be done working and she'd at least get to talk to him one more time before going to sleep.

There wasn't much on that she wanted to watch and she ended up settling on reruns of one of her favorite sitcoms. It was mindless TV and as she ate and half-watched the show, she looked around her living room and began to figure out how she was going to start packing everything up, what she was going to take with her to Atlanta and what she was going to get rid of. Spencer's place was really…unappealing. Not that she'd say that to him.

It was just a little too modern and…bare. Not her style at all. But since she was moving in there, she needed to bring things that would work with what he had.

And that wasn't much.

Hopefully it wouldn't be long before she could bring up the topic of moving to a place they both chose.

Maybe.

His job was in downtown Atlanta and so was his condo. The commute was short and she wondered if he would be open to moving outside the city and into a place that wasn't so…urban. Maybe they could even find a house of their own with a yard. That had her thinking about some of the neighborhoods around Raleigh in which she always envisioned herself living. Her condo was in North Raleigh and it wasn't nearly as built up as all of the areas she'd seen near Atlanta. They were going to have to talk about that and figure out an eventual compromise.

Add that to the list…

It was a little after nine when her phone rang and she smiled when she saw his picture on the screen.

"Hey, you," she said. "I was getting worried."

"How come?"

"My calls kept going to voicemail. Then I felt bad because clearly I kept you from a lot of work this weekend if it meant you were on the phone so much as soon as I left."

He laughed softly. "It wasn't so bad. It was a call that I knew I would have to take and I thought

I'd be done sooner but…"

"It's okay," she said, relaxing on the sofa and enjoying the sound of his voice. "Is it wrong that I miss you already?"

"Not at all. I miss you too. How was your flight?"

They talked for an hour and by that time, Penny was exhausted and ready for bed. She kept her phone with her and put it on speaker as she got undressed and went through her whole routine. It was silly but…it was comforting to listen to Spencer talk to her as she did it. When she slid under the blankets, she took the phone off of speaker and kept it close to her ear as she got ready to wish him a good night.

"What's your day like tomorrow?" he asked softly, soothingly.

"I'm working until six and then I might go to Zumba again. I'm not sure."

"Again, huh? That's a lot of Zumba-ing," he said and then laughed. "Is that how you would describe it?"

She was laughing with him as she said, "You know, I don't know if I've ever heard it put quite that way, but sure. Why not?"

"It's still a lot, Penny."

"I've got nothing else to do after work. Coming home here alone is just…weird now. It never bothered me before we started dating but now when I come home and it's all quiet, it's a little unnerving. So I figured I'd find something to pass the time." She yawned. "Although I should start packing. I know this place isn't very big, but I've utilized every square inch. No doubt it will take a lot of time to start sorting through everything."

He made a non-committal sound.

"I kind of dread going through some of the boxes that I have in storage," she went on. "Some of those things I put in storage to avoid dealing with them after I moved out of my parents' house. Eventually they're going to have to be dealt with." Another yawn. "Either way, I guess that's something to do to pass the time."

"You could go out with a friend or visit your family," he suggested. "You're already on your feet for over eight hours a day so you don't need to add a workout or packing to that."

It was sweet of him to be concerned, but unnecessary, which is what she told him.

"I just worry about you, that's all," he said, his voice getting even softer and it had her relaxing even more and snuggling down under her blankets. "Get some sleep and I'll talk to you tomorrow. Call me when you get home, okay?"

"Mmm-hmm…"

"Love you, beautiful girl."

"Mmm…love you too."

Tuesday was a little more chaotic than usual and Penny ended up splitting her time between the bridal shop and the tuxedo shop. At this rate, she'd be as at ease with groomsmen as she was with the bride and bridal parties. After spending two hours assisting Martin with a large party of groomsmen, she walked back into the bridal shop and went straight to Hailey's office.

"Okay, I need a minute," she said with a huff as she walked in.

And immediately came up short when she noticed all four of her bosses – and Mrs. J – sitting there.

"Oh…sorry. I didn't realize you were having a meeting," she said nervously as she took a few steps back towards the door.

"No, it's okay, Penny," Hailey said with a smile. "We were actually waiting for you."

That was…odd. "Um…is everything all right? Was I gone too long? Because really, Martin needs someone to teach him about scheduling and staffing because I don't think he gets that this isn't a one-man operation. Or that I don't work for him."

"We're working on that," Angie said. "We're going to be finding him additional staff and bringing in someone to assist him with a refresher course on small business management. Hopefully this will be the last time you – or any of us – have to run down and help him."

"Oh…well…that's good. Great," she said and felt like everyone was still just staring at her. "So…you wanted to see me?"

"We did," Hailey said. "Why don't you have a seat?"

Looking over her shoulder towards the sales floor, she was just about to ask who was watching it when Mrs. J spoke.

"Melanie is out there holding down the fort, so to speak, and we don't have any appointments from now until closing. If anyone comes in, she knows to come and get one of us."

Glancing down at her watch, she saw it was only a little after four and they were going to be open until six so…it was clear they were going to keep her back here for a while. When she finally took her seat, she let out a slow breath and tried to calm her nervous heartbeat.

"First of all, breathe," Hailey said with a sympathetic smile. "You look like you're about to have a panic attack."

"I think I am," she admitted. "I had no idea you were calling a meeting today."

Mrs. James reached over and patted her knee. "It was a spur of the moment decision."

That did nothing to calm her anxiety. Were they gathering here to try to talk to her about when she was leaving? About transitioning her out so they could train somebody new? Oh, God…she wasn't ready for that! She knew she needed to be, but now that it was happening it made her heart hurt. These women were her friends and she'd been with them for almost two years! That was a long time and…and the thought of not seeing them every day was almost like how it felt knowing she wouldn't be seeing her family every week or…or…

And now she *was* having a panic attack.

"Oh Lord, do we have a paper bag around she can breathe into?" Angie asked as she stood up.

"No…it's okay," Penny said, hand over her heart, as she took a steadying breath and forced herself to calm down. "I'm fine. Sorry."

It took a minute before it looked like anyone

believed her, but Angie sat back down and offered her a cup of tea and motioned to the tray of cookies and muffins.

Becca smiled. "You should try the chocolate chip banana muffins. They're addictive."

"I don't know," Angie said, studying the tray of goodies. "Those brownies look pretty decadent."

"Can someone make me a plate of fruit?" Ella asked, snuggling her son close. "And maybe hand me a bottle of water?"

It took a few minutes for everyone to take what they wanted and get comfortable again. It wasn't until Penny had taken a sip of her tea and a bite of her muffin that Hailey started to speak.

"We were waiting for you because we have some updates on the complex and wanted your input."

"Um…my input? Why? You know that I'm…you know…" *Ugh.* She couldn't even bring herself to say it because she knew she'd get worked up all over again. "I don't think I should get to voice anything where this is concerned."

"Oh, shut up," Angie said. "You've been with us for so long and you know almost as much about what we're trying to do here as the rest of us. We trust your opinion."

"It's true," Becca said. "Even when you were only modeling in the shows, you had a grasp on what needed to be done and were always helping out and offering suggestions that we ended up using."

"And you've put time in with each of the businesses so really…I think you – almost more than any of us – is entitled to an opinion," Ella added.

Well damn. That just made her heart squeeze even more.

Don't cry…don't cry…don't cry…

"So…what kind of updates are you looking at?" she asked, forcing herself to at least try and sound like she wasn't ready to fall apart at the thought of not being here to see any of it.

"You know we built this space with the idea that we were going to expand," Mrs. James began. "Like a mall, there are several more store spaces that need to be filled. Besides what we have here already – the gowns, the tuxes, the coffee shop, florist and photographer – we just met with a lovely young woman who does wedding and event invitations and party favors."

Unable to help herself, Penny smiled and thought about how much fun that shop would be to work in. Why couldn't that place have been here already? It sounded like the kind of place she wouldn't have minded helping out in. "That sounds wonderful! And she'd be able to do probably so much more, right? Calligraphy, bridal party swag, seating charts and cards, wedding programs…wow. That's going to be a great addition!"

The five women around her all smiled.

"She came to us with her ideas and we thought it would be a perfect fit," Hailey said. "But that's not all…"

O-kay…

"I've gotten a lot of inquiries from brides looking for caterers for their showers and parties,"

Becca began. "And while I can certainly provide them with some names and even do some small stuff if they only want desserts, but we thought it might be nice to expand my shop to include a café that served sandwiches, salads and that kind of fare and then be able to offer more to people looking for casual catering."

"Oh, wow! Now that is exciting!" Penny cried. "You'll have to move your location though, right? I know you have that double space further toward the back – which would mess with your prime spot where you are now – but if people came in and were lured by the yummy smells coming from the café, they'd be more apt to walk through the mall and see everything that we have to offer so…really…it's a win-win situation."

More smiles.

"That's the plan," Hailey said, "and we've met with someone who will handle more of the food and catering part of the business who will partner with Becca – almost like they're renting the space from her even though they're sharing it."

"I'm not a caterer," Becca added. "I can bake just fine and do the small stuff, but cooking for the masses is too overwhelming."

"It's good to know your strengths," Ella said as she cradled baby Devin in her arms.

"We've had a few other inquiries as well," Mrs. James chimed in. "Not all of them were the right fit – a DJ, a limousine company, tent rentals…" She smiled even as she shook her head. "Those are all under the umbrella of things you would need for a wedding, but there's no need for them to have a storefront here. We already have them at our bridal fairs where they have tables for people to get information, but they're not a good fit for what we're trying to build here."

Penny nodded.

"As we've grown, there's been a lot of interest from local businesses who want to get in and rent space from us," Hailey explained, "but we're trying to be smart about our choices and make sure that everyone here fits with our business plan and ideals."

"We probably should have done a better job with Martin," Angie murmured and there was a collective "Amen to that."

"What are you going to do with the spot Becca's vacating?" Penny asked. "It would be a shame to leave that space vacant so close to the front entrance. You don't want people seeing that when they first walk in…" She stopped and gasped – her hand instantly flying up to cover her mouth. "Sorry. That was rude of me. I'm sure you already have a plan."

Luckily, no one was offended. If anything, they all laughed.

"We thought of that too," Hailey explained. "Of course, while we are dismantling the café and moving the equipment over, there isn't a whole lot we can do to hide the construction. We'll do as much as we can overnight to keep the dust and noise to a minimum."

"Of course," Penny agreed.

"There will be barriers in place so clients and potential clients won't have to look at the construction mess," Mrs. James said. "Sort of like when you go to an amusement park and they have ten-foot walls blocking off an area so you can't see what they're building. We'll have those up with the Enchanted logo and a promise of more wedding magic coming soon or something to that effect."

Taking another bite of her muffin, Penny looked at Hailey.

"We have a couple of options for the space, but there's one that we're leaning toward," Hailey went on as she reached behind her desk. "We have the plans all drawn up, but we wanted your input."

With a shrug, Penny placed her plate and cup down on the coffee table and reached for the poster board Hailey was holding out to her. Once she set it right, she scanned it. It was a mechanical drawing of the space without a lot of obvious ways of telling what the spot was going to be used for.

All of the plumbing was staying in place...there looked like there were going to be some stations for sitting as well as a waiting area...

She looked up at the girls in confusion. "I don't get it. This doesn't say what you're making and some of these details are written in such a small font that I can't read it."

"Oh...I must have given you the wrong one," Hailey said with a small chuckle. "There's so many things going on, it's a wonder I can keep track of them all. I feel like such a scatterbrain."

Which was odd of her to say because Hailey was one of the most meticulously organized people Penny had ever met.

Glancing back at the drawing, she began to see

it for what it was…a salon. Someone else was going to come in here and take her spot. Her dream.

Tears instantly began to blur her vision and she did her best to keep her gaze averted as she wiped at her eyes.

Dammit.

Dammit, dammit, dammit!

Without looking up, she took the new poster board from Hailey's hand. Clearing her throat, she looked at it and it was exactly as she had envisioned her salon being – everything from the placement of the stations to the light fixtures, the color scheme, the…

She looked up at Hailey. "So you're going with a salon?" she forced herself to say.

All Hailey did was nod.

"Who's the occupant going to be? Obviously you've met with them if you have the plans here." That looked suspiciously a lot like the ones she had shared with them. "I mean, you must have someone selected if you already have the plans drawn up."

And dammit, she hated the tremor in her voice.

Maybe these women weren't her friends after all because this was just…it was mean. It was one thing to ask her opinion on the other additions to the business, but to make her sit here and talk about someone else having her spot, her business, her dream…that was too much. How could she have misjudged them so badly? And how was she supposed to sit here and calmly have this conversation when all she wanted to do was storm out?

This definitely made leaving a whole lot easier…

"You know we wanted you to have the salon for your glam squad," Hailey said, seemingly oblivious to Penny's despair. "And we would have gladly funded it for you."

She held up a hand to stop her. "I know you did and I appreciate that. This was something I felt very strongly about. I needed it to be mine – something that I owned on my own."

"We know," Mrs. James said, "and we respect that."

"However," Hailey went on, "you really brought to our attention how much having an on-site salon would improve what we've already created here. Besides having someone on staff – so to speak – to help with the fashion shows, it would also be a perk for brides to be able to come in and try on gowns and have someone available to discuss hair and makeup with them so there are no last-minute surprises."

"Remember Donna Kyle? The bride who ordered the massively – overly – beaded gown and then chose to wear her long hair down?" Angie asked. "Remember how she came in and complained because no one told her how her hair was going to constantly snag on all of the beading?"

"That should have been obvious," Penny murmured. "But yes, I remember that."

"She was a nightmare and for a while there, the way she kept calling and complaining bordered on harassment," Becca commented. "I thought we were going to have to get some sort of order of protection to keep her away."

"I don't think it was quite that dramatic. However, if we had a style consultant on staff, we could avoid things like that and offer brides appointments with the salon to discuss all of these things," Hailey expanded. "And if it were someone who had a working knowledge of the gowns, then all the better."

Wait a minute…was she saying that this person – this…this…dream-stealer already worked here at Enchanted? She looked over her shoulder toward the showroom and glared at Melanie. Not once had the girl ever mentioned having a cosmetology license and now she was going to have her own glam squad? How was that fair? All of this was exactly the kind of stuff she had wanted to do! And it sucked that someone else – Melanie - was now going to get to do it!

"Anyway," Hailey went on, "the new owner of the shop is here and I know this is asking a lot, but we'd really appreciate it if you could take a few minutes and talk with them."

Penny's eyes went wide with disbelief.

Meet with them? Was Hailey serious? Why not just bring Melanie back here when this whole damn meeting started? Why make such a dramatic production out of it?

"We realize that – all things considered – you might not be comfortable doing it," Mrs. James said sympathetically, "but your vision for it was just so spot on and as much as I think this new person gets it, it would be helpful if maybe you could just…talk about how you saw things going."

Getting up and storming out wasn't an option. No matter how appealing it was.

She'd kick and scream and cry later when she got home. She'd call Spencer and tell him and then do everything she could to start the moving process as soon as possible. With her stomach clenching and her heart racing, Penny forced herself to look at each of the women as she said, "Sure. If you think that will help, then that will be fine."

Immediately, she stood up, smoothed down her skirt and waited. Everyone else rose and Becca and Ella were the first to walk out. Followed by Angie.

"I'm just going to go grab us some fresh tea," Mrs. James said. "Hailey? You'll show our guest in, right?"

Guest? Couldn't they just say Melanie? And just like that, Penny was alone in the office with her head spinning. She had dropped both poster boards to the floor earlier and she bent down to pick them up so she didn't seem disrespectful.

Even though right now what she wanted to do was tear them both up.

And maybe light them on fire.

Then spit on them.

"I was hoping you'd have on the red heels today," a male voice said from behind her.

Spinning around, she was shocked to find Spencer standing there.

And Hailey smiling as she closed the office door.

"Spencer," she said breathlessly. "What are you doing here?"

He gave her a sheepish grin as he stepped

further into the room. With his hands in his pockets, he let out a breath. "Well, something's happened."

Her stomach dropped. She reached out and placed a hand on his arm, thinking the news had to be bad for him to be here like this with no warning. "Oh my God? What's happened?"

"I lost my job," he said, his voice and expression somber.

"Wait? What?" she cried. "I mean…how? You've been working so hard and…and…is it because of me? Is it because of all the time you've been spending in Raleigh?"

He nodded. "It was."

And then she felt terrible. Could this day get any worse?

"Oh, Spencer, I am so sorry!" She stepped in close and hugged him. "I don't even know what to say. What are you going to do now?"

He sighed as he wrapped his arms around her. "Well, I had some time to think about it and…I think it's all going to be okay. I've invested in a business. You know, something to hold me over until I find a job."

She pulled back. "You invested…? Wait…um…what? I'm totally confused."

Spencer released her and walked over to where she had dropped the plans on the floor. Again. He picked them up and placed one back on Hailey's desk and then studied the other. He leaned on the desk and asked her to join him.

"I'm trying my hand at something new," he began. "I realized that there is a lot more to the architectural and design field than what I've been doing." He studied the plans again and smiled. "I had forgotten how much fun things like this were."

"Wait a minute," she said. "Are you telling me that you designed this?"

He nodded, and it took Penny a minute for all the pieces to come together.

A slow smile played at her lips. "And is this particular salon the business that you've invested in?"

He nodded again.

She took the designs from his hand and sighed dramatically. "It's an interesting design. The colors are good and I think it's a great use of space."

"Thanks," he said, sounding very pleased.

Then she sighed dramatically. "I sure hope you can find someone to run this place, because I'm moving to Atlanta so…"

The plans were quickly taken away from her and she found herself in Spencer's arms and his lips claimed hers before she could even blink. Nothing had ever felt sweeter. She melted against him as the enormity of what he'd just told her started to sink in.

Then she broke the kiss.

"Holy crap! Are you telling me that you bought the space and that it's for me?"

He laughed, a deep, rich sound that had her tingling all over. "Actually, I thought I was kissing you and pretty much telling you that I love you, but…before that…yes. That's exactly what I was saying."

"Oh my God!" she cried excitedly as she moved away. "Oh my God! I was sitting here with the girls and thinking that they were the meanest people ever for making me talk to the person who was going to own my dream! You have no idea how upset I was!"

He chuckled and reached for her hand. "We thought you might feel that way, but I knew once you realized what was happening, you'd be okay." Then he studied her. "Are you? Are you mad that I did this? I remember how you turned the girls down, but I was hoping if it were me and it was something for us – for our future – then you wouldn't mind too much."

"Are you kidding me? I…I'm so incredibly blown away by this, Spencer," she began. "But seriously, what about your job? If we do this, then I'm staying here. And if you're in Atlanta then…"

He squeezed her hand. "I really did lose my job." When she gasped, he continued. "It was by choice," he explained. "I talked to my bosses about what was going on and they were sympathetic to a point, but ultimately we thought it best if I came here and…worked on other projects."

She looked at him curiously. "Other projects? What does that mean?"

Tugging her in close, he kissed her again before answering. "It means that there is a division of my company that works right out of this area and on top of that, my father is selling his firm and they're hiring as well."

"Wait…wouldn't that be counterproductive to what you both wanted? You'd still be working there, so why not own it?"

His arms tightened around her. "Because I don't want to own it. I don't want to work sixty-hours a week or more the way he has. I want to have a life and I want to be able to do the kind of work that I love and by working for someone else, I can. Actually, I'm kind of a big deal right now. Big demand," he teased.

"Yes you are," she purred and rested her head right over his heart. "Can we go and look at the space now? I've been totally patient about it, right?"

"In a minute," he said and held her close for a little longer. "Actually, there's something rather important that we need to talk about."

Raising her head, she said, "We do?"

Nodding he replied, "We do."

Penny looked at him expectantly.

"Do you remember the day I dropped you off at the Atlanta airport?"

"Uh-huh."

"Do you remember what we said?"

She looked at him oddly. "Um…about how much I didn't want to leave, how I didn't want to wait on that long security line…I asked to stay…"

He chuckled softly and tucked a finger under her chin. "That day we said I love you for the first time."

Gasping, she said, "We did?"

"We sure did." Smiling down at her, he caressed her cheek. "And we've been pretty much saying it regularly and we never made a big deal about it. And we should have."

"Oh," she said with a breathy sigh.

"Penny Blake, I love you so much. We've spent a lot of time getting to this place – and not just here at Enchanted, but here together," he said softly. "I feel like after all the stopping and starting, we always came back to this. To us. I don't want to stop again. I want this to keep going. You have always been it for me, always the girl for me. I wish I had said it to you sooner and not waited until we were in the middle of a crowded airport."

Tears streamed down her face at his words. "I think I waited my whole life to hear you tell me you loved me," she admitted, "and I can't believe that it came so naturally and at such an odd time that I didn't even realize it. Maybe because it's how I always felt that it came out like that." Pausing as he wiped away her tears, she smiled at him. "And I agree, no more stopping. You and I were always meant to be and I feel like the luckiest girl in the world right now. I love you."

She didn't get to say another word because he was kissing her and if they weren't in the middle of Hailey's office, she would have let it go a lot further. When Spencer lifted his head, he grinned at her. "They may not have cameras in here, but if we stay in here much longer, I'm pretty sure they're going to know what we're doing."

Laughing, she swatted at him playfully. "Spoilsport."

"You'll thank me later when no one is giving you knowing looks," he teased. "Now come on, I thought you wanted to see your new business space. Geez...how long am I supposed to wait?"

With another laugh, he led her from the office and they were met by Hailey, Angie, Becca, Ella and Mrs. James who were all smiling from ear to ear. After a round of hugs and congratulations, Hailey stopped them before they could leave.

"There's one more thing we need to do before you go down and inspect your spot," Hailey said and grinned when Angie handed her a large flat box, which she, in turn, handed to Penny.

"What's this?"

"This is just a little gift that we got for you to welcome you and Glam to the Enchanted Bridal family."

Curious, Penny opened the box and found a large mounted poster with the logo she had designed for her business. Looking up at the five of them – and Spencer – she was overcome with emotion. "I…I don't even know what to say. This is one of the most thoughtful gifts I ever could have asked for."

"Come on," Spencer said. "Let's go see where we can hang that."

Then they all walked together to Becca's coffee shop which would soon be the home of Penny's glam squad studio.

She was home.

EPILOGUE

Six months later…

"I kind of feel like we shouldn't be doing this."

"Nonsense. It's totally fine."

"It's a little unnecessary."

"Unnecessary or…sexy?"

Spencer laughed as he let Penny tug him along through the darkened mall of Enchanted Bridal. It was after hours and everything else was closed, but tomorrow was the grand opening of Glam by Penny and she wanted to come in and look over everything one last time and wanted him here with her. They were on their way for a late dinner when she asked if they could stop by.

"Sexy?" he repeated. "I thought I was just here to make sure there wasn't any lingering construction dust."

"Silly man," she murmured as she unlocked the gate to her shop.

Their shop.

Ever since that day six months ago when he'd presented her with the plans for the salon, things had moved at a frantic pace. Work on the new coffee shop had started immediately and they were lucky that Angie's husband was in construction and was able to get a crew in to get started. Once they had stripped the shop, Spencer moved in with a hired crew to start working. It made more sense to have two crews working at the same time rather than waiting to get started.

The end result was the salon of Penny's dreams.

She opened the gate and stepped in, then motioned for him to follow before she closed it behind him. There were just a few security lights on but even in the dim light he knew the place was spectacular – nothing out of place and beyond clean. They had a cleaning crew in there earlier in the day, which is why he had to ask…

"Why are we here again?"

She sighed. "I told you. I just want to make sure everything's in its place and ready for tomorrow." She was practically bouncing on her toes now. "Look at this place! It's perfect!" Then she flung herself into his arms and kissed him until he was completely breathless. When she broke the kiss, she grinned at him. "And it's all because of you. You made this happen!"

But Spencer shook his head and put a little space between them. "Nuh-uh…*we* made this happen. You had the dream and the vision; I just helped put it in motion."

Penny smiled at him. "We make a great team."

He nodded. "Yes, we do. And this place? This is going to help secure our future."

She waved him off. "I don't know about that, but I think it's going to be a great start." Turning, she looked around the space again and when she turned back to him, he was down on one knee. Gasping with surprise, her hands flew to her mouth before she said. "Ohmygod…"

"Penny Blake, I said my vows with you for the first time when I was eight years old, and I'm hoping that you'll say them with me again. This time, in front of all of our family and friends and not just my sister."

"Spencer," she said shakily, sinking down to her knees in front of him. "What are you doing?"

Pulling out the ring he'd had in his pocket all day, he held it out to her. "I love you. I've always loved you. And as we're getting ready to start this new chapter of our lives with Glam, I thought tonight would be the perfect night to do this." He gazed at her lovingly. "I had planned on doing it at dinner, but now that we're here, I thought it was fitting to ask you – in this space – to be my wife. This is where we realized we make great business partners, and I know we'll find that we make even better lifelong partners – husband and wife." He paused and took her left hand in his. "Will you marry me?"

She nodded her head vigorously as her eyes filled with tears. He slid the ring on her finger before rising. "Spencer Buchanan, I have waited a lifetime for you and I would love to be your wife."

Then pulled her closely to kiss her.

Minutes later, breathless, they broke apart.

"Um...do you remember the night you came in for your tux and lost your keys?" Penny asked softly.

A slow grin crossed Spencer's face. Remember it? Hell, it was still one of his hottest dreams of her. "Of course I do."

"Well...I was thinking...maybe...we could christen this space tonight. You know, really make it ours."

He quickly jumped to his feet and grabbed one of her hands and immediately tugged her to her feet. "I know just the spot."

Laughing, they made their way to the small office space Penny had set up in the back room and thoroughly christened the space.

And it marked the beginning of just one of many adventures yet to come.

ABOUT THE AUTHOR

Samantha Chase is a New York Times and USA Today bestseller of contemporary romance. She released her debut novel in 2011 and currently has more than forty titles under her belt! When she's not working on a new story, she spends her time reading romances, playing way too many games of Scrabble or Solitaire on Facebook, wearing a tiara while playing with her sassy pug Maylene...oh, and spending time with her husband of 25 years and their two sons in North Carolina.

Where to Find Me:
Website: www.chasing-romance.com
Facebook:
www.facebook.com/SamanthaChaseFanClub
Twitter: https://twitter.com/SamanthaChase3
Amazon: http://amzn.to/2lhrtQa
Sign up for my mailing list and get exclusive content and chances to win members-only prizes!
http://bit.ly/1jqdxPR

Also by Samantha Chase

The Enchanted Bridal Series:

The Wedding Season
Friday Night Brides
The Bridal Squad

The Montgomery Brothers Series:

Wait for Me
Trust in Me
Stay with Me
More of Me
Return to You
Meant for You
I'll Be There
Until There Was Us

The Shaughnessy Brothers Series:

Made for Us
Love Walks In
Always My Girl
This is Our Song
Sky Full of Stars
Holiday Spice

Band on the Run Series:

One More Kiss
One More Promise
One More Moment

The Christmas Cottage Series:

The Christmas Cottage
Ever After

Silver Bell Falls Series:

Christmas in Silver Bell Falls
Christmas On Pointe
A Very Married Christmas

Life, Love & Babies Series:

The Baby Arrangement
Baby, Be Mine
Baby, I'm Yours

Preston's Mill Series:

Roommating
Speed Dating
Complicating

The Protectors Series:

Protecting His Best Friend's Sister
Protecting the Enemy
Protecting the Girl Next Door
Protecting the Movie Star

7 Brides for 7 Soldiers

Ford

Standalone Novels:

Jordan's Return
Catering to the CEO
In the Eye of the Storm
A Touch of Heaven
Moonlight in Winter Park
Wildest Dreams
Going My Way
Going to Be Yours
Waiting for Midnight
Seeking Forever
Mistletoe Between Friends
Snowflake Inn

NEW YORK TIMES BESTSELLING AUTHOR

SAMANTHA
CHASE

THE WEDDING
Season

Enjoy the following excerpt for

The Wedding Season

The Enchanted Bride Series Book One

PROLOGUE

Fifteen years ago...

Tricia Patterson nervously approached the closed classroom door. Her heart was beating wildly in her chest and she had to stop and take a few steadying breaths. This wasn't anything new.

The way her family moved around, you'd think she'd be used to this by now.

New home.

New school.

And repeat.

Unfortunately, it never got any easier. The anxiety, the nerves, the fear of not fitting in. Most of the time it worked out all right. She'd make new friends, but in the back of her mind she knew it wouldn't be long until she had to pack up and move again.

But not anymore.

Thanks to her parents' divorce, Tricia wouldn't have to move again. She and her mom had found a place in a small town on the east coast of Long Island and they wouldn't have to pack up and move unless they wanted to.

She really hoped they wouldn't want to any time soon.

It had taken a couple of days to get unpacked and settled in, and today her mom had finally brought her to the local high school to get registered. Secretly, Tricia had hoped to drag out the process a little bit longer, but no such luck. She was here, registered, had her locker assigned and her schedule freshly printed out.

There was no turning back.

Looking down, she stared at the schedule for at least the tenth time in as many minutes. "It's just homeroom," she muttered. "Nothing to do except sit and wait until the first bell. You can do this."

With a steadying breath, she reached for the door, turned the handle and opened it.

Twenty-five pairs of eyes were instantly on her and her breakfast threatened to make a reappearance.

"May I help you?" the teacher asked. She was an older woman – maybe in her sixties – but she had a kind smile.

"Um...I'm Tricia Patterson," she said softly as she walked toward the desk. "I just transferred here and..." Reaching into her one binder, she pulled out her paperwork and handed it to the teacher.

"Welcome, Tricia. I'm Mrs. O'Keefe," she said, still smiling. "Why don't you take a seat for now? I'll rework the seating arrangement for tomorrow, but for now, feel free to sit at one of the empty desks."

"Thank you," Tricia mumbled and turned around. Okay, now there were only twenty-four people staring at her and it was still pretty damn intimidating. Scanning the room, she located an empty desk in the back corner, quickly made her way over and sat down.

After a minute, everyone seemed to lose interest in her and Tricia breathed a sigh of relief. She pulled out the papers they had given her down in the office and found a map of the school to show how to get from one class to the next. She was studying it when all of a sudden...

"Hey! I'm Sean Peterson."

To her right, there was a boy, Sean, leaning over smiling at her. She glanced at him and wasn't sure how to respond. Was he being nice? Sincere? Or was he someone she should avoid? Lord knows she'd dealt with that sort of thing in each school. It never failed that there was at least one person who seemed to genuinely want to befriend her only to turn out to be a freak in some way, shape or form.

"Hi," she muttered and went back to studying the map.

"So, you just transferred here? From where?" he asked.

Mentally she rolled her eyes. Placing the paperwork back down, she turned her head and looked at him. "From Rochester."

"Really? Upstate, huh? That's cool." He straightened and smiled and Tricia had to admit he seemed really nice. And he was kind of cute. Sandy brown hair, brown eyes and a nice smile. "When did you move?"

"Over the weekend," Tricia said but didn't know what else to add to her short response.

"Awesome. Where in town? I live over off of Barnford. I don't know if you know where that is but…"

"It's right by where we live, too," Tricia said, hating how she sounded so excited at the information. "I mean, we actually live on Barnford. The house on the corner of Barnford and Grove."

"Seriously?" Sean asked, his smile growing. "You mean the white house with the red shutters?"

Tricia nodded.

"I'm actually a block over," he said. "I'm on the opposite side of the street, on the corner of Barnford and Elm."

"No way!"

"Totally serious." He twisted in his seat so he was facing Tricia. "Do you have your schedule?"

She pulled it from her pile of papers and handed it to him. "This is the part I hate the most. Trying to find the classrooms and figuring out who to sit with."

"Well that's easy," Sean said. "Your schedule is almost identical to mine." He looked up at her again, his brown eyes smiling. "Just stick with me and I'll get you to all of them and then you can sit by me."

Tricia almost sagged with relief. "I...I appreciate it."

"There's just one problem," he said, his expression going almost comically serious.

"What?"

"I don't know your name. I mean, I know you said it when you walked it, but I didn't really hear it. I don't mind walking with you to classes, but I figure you'd prefer it if I didn't call you 'Hey, you' all day."

Tricia couldn't help but giggle. "I'm Tricia. Tricia Patterson."

Sean's smile was back. "It's nice to meet you, Tricia." Then he leaned in as if he had a secret to tell her. "With you being Patterson and my last name being Peterson, I think we're going to be stuck with each other all through high school. It's a good thing we became friends now."

And in that moment, Tricia couldn't agree more.

ONE

"You have *got* to be kidding me," Tricia grumbled as she sorted through the mail that was just delivered. She considered running down the block after her mailman and throwing it all back at him and shaking him until he promised to be more considerate, but then thought better of it. After all, it wasn't his fault she was a single woman.

A single woman who was currently holding three wedding invitations in her hand.

Cursing under her breath, she made her way back up the driveway and into her house, slamming the door behind her. Tossing the pile on her little entryway table without opening it, she walked through to the kitchen to get a drink. The sound of her phone ringing stopped her.

Her foul mood was instantly forgotten when she saw Sean's name on the screen. "Hey! It's you!"

"Hey, beautiful," Sean said with a small chuckle. "How are you doing?"

Walking into the living room, she collapsed on the couch. "Okay…and you?"

"By the sound of your voice, I'd say you are officially lying to me. So what's going on, Patterson?"

She rolled her eyes, hating how he rarely called her by her first name. "Three more came today."

"You're kidding!"

"Do I sound like I'm kidding?"

Sean chuckled again. "How is this even possible? How could it be that almost everyone we know is getting married this summer? Didn't they all get married last summer?"

"That's what I thought," she mumbled and threw her head back with a sigh. "I'm telling you, Sean, I'm nailing the mailbox shut as soon as we're off the phone!" The two of them had been commiserating over the last week about the upcoming wedding season.

"Tampering with the mail is a federal offense," he joked and Tricia couldn't help but smile.

"I'm not tampering with the mail, per se. It's my mailbox and if I want it nailed shut then…"

"Relax," he said smoothly. "Besides, how many more invites could there possibly be? I don't think we know any more people."

"I don't know. I have a feeling we're still missing some."

"Sure but…what are the odds of those people getting married this summer too? As it is, we're up to what? Five weddings? Six?"

"Today's mail brought us up to six."

"Yikes."

"Exactly." It really was a little more than Tricia wanted to deal with. She was feeling like the proverbial "always a bridesmaid, never a bride" while Sean had complained about how he was tired of people trying to set him up with their "cute" sisters or cousins. "Seriously, we don't have to go to all of them, do we?"

"I mean I guess we don't have to," Sean began, "but…they are all our friends. Whose would we skip?"

Standing, Tricia quickly went over and grabbed

today's invitations and then walked to the kitchen to grab the three that had arrived the previous week before sitting back down on the sofa. "Okay, let's think about this. The first one is Tami and Eric on June third." She paused. "Actually, I'd really like to go to that one. They're a great couple and have always been good friends to me."

"Ditto," Sean said. "Next?"

"Linda and Jerry on the fifth. Wow. It's going to be a very full weekend."

"Yeah, but…if we do one, we kind of have to do the other. It will be all the same people and how would we explain going to one and not the other?"

"Good point," Tricia conceded. "Give me a minute to open these new ones and see if any of the dates overlap."

"Wishful thinking, Patterson. Our luck is never that good."

"You know, I can't help but notice how you keep talking about all these events in the plural sense. Does that mean you're definitely going to be back home for the summer?"

"That's the plan," Sean said, and Tricia could hear the smile in his voice. For the last year, Sean had been working as a contractor over in the Middle East and Asia, helping to rebuild areas that were torn apart by war and a tsunami. It was hard work but she knew Sean loved it.

"And you want to spend your free time when you finally get home going to weddings? Seriously?" she asked with a laugh. "What's wrong with you?"

"Well, although it will cost me a fortune, it's a

great opportunity to see everyone at one shot and get caught up."

It made sense. "Okay, next up we have...Donna and Jason on..." She scanned the invitation, "the eleventh. That's almost too much, right? Can we skip that one?"

"You can, but I can't. Jason and I played soccer together since we were five. I have to be there."

"Are you sure you're even invited? How often do you check your mail?" She asked with as serious of a tone as she could manage, but Sean knew immediately she was teasing.

"Ha-ha, very funny. I get my mail on a regular basis and although I haven't gotten today's mail – and probably won't until next week – I'm fairly certain I'm invited to all the same weddings as you."

"Fine, whatever. Don't get all defensive." She shuffled through the mail and opened up the rest of the invites. "It looks like we get a break for a couple of weeks and the next batch doesn't start up again until the second week of July."

"So that means we don't have to make any firm decisions right now then."

"You don't, but I do. The first one up in July is Kristen and Bobby. I told her I couldn't commit to being in the bridal party but that I'd be there."

"Okay, fine. Bobby was also on the soccer team so I should be there too."

"You know high school was over ten years ago, right? It doesn't matter that you played on a team together – it doesn't obligate you to stuff for the rest of your life," she said.

"You wouldn't understand," he replied. "We were all close and once I started traveling, I've missed out on a lot. My friends mean a lot to me – you should know that – and as much as it pains me to have to dress up and do the chicken dance, I want to be there for my friends."

Suddenly, Tricia didn't feel quite as antagonistic toward the invitations. "You're right," she sighed. "I guess there's a part of me that just dreads all that goes with accepting the invites."

"You mean the inevitable attempts to fix you up with someone?"

"That and the pity looks I get. And I get a lot of them. You know…the old 'Poor Tricia. You'll find someone soon. I'm sure of it.' I hate those looks."

"Yeah well, I'd take pity over pimps."

She couldn't help but laugh. "Is that what we're calling it now?"

"Might as well. It's pretty much what they're doing," Sean said and then sighed loudly. "I don't know maybe it's not…" He stopped. "Wait a minute," he began excitedly. "I've got it! I know exactly how to get us out of those situations!"

"I'm listening…" she said hopefully.

"We go together."

All of the hope she was just feeling quickly deflated from her body. "That's it? That's your big plan? How is that going to get us out of anything? Everyone is used to seeing us together. And considering you've been out of the country for so damn long, they'll just figure you didn't have time to find a date and so you asked me. I'll be the pity date!" She cursed. "Damn it! I can't escape it!"

"No, no, no…listen. We go together as like, you know, a couple."

She shook her head. "No one is going to believe it."

"Sure they will. We'll get all cozy and you'll have to look at me as if you adore me – which shouldn't be hard to do – and hang on my every word."

"You're crazy, you know that? I'm not going to hang on your every word and whatever else. It's ridiculous and it won't work."

"Why not? You're telling me you can't pretend to be in love with me for a couple of hours? I'm crushed."

"Don't be such a drama queen, Sean," she said wearily. "It's not just a couple of hours. We're looking at potentially six weddings at six-to-eight hours each with people who've known us for years. It's going to take a lot more than batting my eyelashes at you while holding your hand."

"What have we got to lose?" he asked. "Unless…unless you had someone else you planned on going with."

Unfortunately, she didn't. It had been months since she'd even been on a date. But there was no need to dwell on it right now. "No, that's not it. I just don't think…"

"C'mon, Tricia. It makes perfect sense. We'll test out the theory at the first wedding and see how it goes. I'm sure no one's going to expect us to be pawing at each other to prove we're in a relationship. What do you say?"

"I still think you're crazy but…"

"Look, it's not that big of a deal and I guarantee you we'll have a lot more fun this way. We'll shock everyone and then field all kinds of questions and then we'll get to enjoy ourselves. No ducking behind potted plants or running into the bathroom to avoid the feeding frenzy of well-meaning people who claim only to be thinking of our happiness."

Tricia took a minute to think about it and as much as she believed they'd never be able to pull it off, it was certainly worth a try. "You're right. Damn it."

"Excellent!"

"So that leads me to our other order of business, where you'll be staying while you're home. I hope it's here." Tricia was actually renting Sean's childhood home. From the first time she had walked through the front door, she had fallen in love with it. When Sean's mom wanted to move away and travel a bit herself, she had offered it to Tricia. Someday she hoped to own it but wanted to wait until the time was right.

"I wouldn't dream of staying anyplace else," he said. "Where else could I go for free and sleep in my old room?" He paused. "You haven't changed anything in there, have you?" he asked with exaggerated anxiety.

"No, precious," she mocked. "Your Van Halen posters are still on the wall so you can relax. I'll just have to unlock the shrine and air it out before you get here. Which reminds me, when exactly will you be getting home?"

"End of May. I'm thinking the twenty-eighth but figure you'll have to give or take a day with that. Nothing ever goes as planned."

"And what about your mom? Are you going to go and see her first and then come here or the other way around?"

"Honestly? I'm not sure. Probably after the first round of weddings I'll track her down. Last I talked to her she was going on a cruise with some friends and was talking about yoga classes." He sighed. "Why can't she just be like other moms?"

That made Tricia laugh. Stephanie Peterson had never been like other moms – that was one of the things she'd always loved about her. "You have no idea how lucky you are. Steph gets out there and is enjoying her life. My mom prefers to live like a hermit."

"That's not true and you know it," Sean said.

"Which part?"

"Your mom and John are very happy and they have plenty of friends. You need to stop picking on them."

"Hey, same goes for you, buddy. Your mom is very happy and has a lot of friends. She just chooses to have them all over the world. There's nothing wrong with that."

"I guess," he grumbled. "It's just hard to pin her down sometimes. It would be nice to have a home base to go and see her. I'm never sure where I'm going to find her."

"It's not like you've been home a whole lot, Sean," she reminded him. "I don't see why it should bother you so much."

"Yeah, well, it doesn't just bother me. Ryan complains about it too. Every time I talk to him he tells me how it's easier to find Waldo than it is to find Steph."

"Yeah, well...Ryan's just grumpy. I swear, he's always got something to complain about." It was only partially true. Ryan was Sean's older brother and while he and Sean had a great relationship, any time Tricia was around him he seemed to be irritated.

Sean chuckled. "I don't know where you get it from. Ry's not like that. He does his own fair share of traveling but even with that, Steph has him beat."

"I think that's great for her!"

"You women. Always sticking together."

"And don't you forget it." There was a moment of companionable silence before Tricia spoke again. "So you really think you'll be coming home this time?"

"I do. I know I said that six months ago but then the tsunami hit. I was already over here with a team. What was I supposed to do?"

"You don't have to fix the entire world, Sean. You have people back here who love you and want to see you."

"Aww...see? You love me. It's going to be so easy for you to play the part of my girlfriend for these weddings!" he teased.

"You're an idiot," she laughed.

"Yes, yes, yes," he agreed. "But you still love me."

That just made her laugh harder. "Knock it off,

doofus."

"Come on. I'm not completely hideous to look at, am I?"

"Now you're just fishing for compliments. And besides, you've been gone for like two years. For all I know you could look like some kind of yeti now."

"I promise to shave," he said with a laugh. "Admit it. This is going to be so much fun. We can watch all of their shocked faces and we can be as outrageous as we want."

"I'm sure I'm going to regret this at some point, but okay. Fine. I guess it could be kind of fun. Plus, we'll get to spend a whole lot of time together getting caught up."

"So…it's a plan?"

She nodded even though she knew he couldn't see her. "Definitely. I'll take care of all the RSVP'ing for us if you don't mind."

"Be my guest, *sweetheart*," he gushed.

"*Ugh*…knock it off. Save it for the audience."

"You're no fun. How are we supposed to come off as being believable if we don't practice?"

"Sean?"

"Yeah?"

"Let it go. We'll be fine and I don't think either of us is going to have to pull off an Oscar-worthy performance."

"You never know…"

Tricia didn't even want to think about it. All she knew was her best friend was coming home and they'd have a couple of weeks to hang out together. Weddings or no weddings, it was going to be fun!

AMITYVILLE PUBLIC LIBRARY

3 5922 00388 9148

Made in the USA
Middletown, DE
04 January 2020

82419043R00126

AMITYVILLE PUBLIC LIBRARY

JAN 08 2020